Escape

By
Rae Burton

Mom–

Happy Mother's Day 2009
(It's a little late.)

1

In the slums of the city, dark of night, he strolled the streets, side-stepping the many prostitutes that got in the way. Some looked ready to offer services, but he just walked faster. Tonight wasn't the night for fun and games. Tonight there was a job to do. Standing still, he surveyed the crowd. She wasn't here. From the corner he'd spotted her but now she'd vanished. He moved quickly to the alley. If someone had come up to her, she could already be gone and the open opportunity would be gone for another night. It'd been too long already.

It was a struggle to see in the darkened alley but two figures could easily be seen. One was a short man. The other a tall, slender woman, body perfectly silhouetted by the street light. It had to be her. Lucky night. Just not for her or her partner. He slipped on the black leather gloves, tugged on a hat. Head ducked. Each step closer to the target. One shot.

*****

Alarm blaring. Six o'clock. Every day she hit snooze twice, not getting out of bed until six-thirty. The perfect target. She got out of bed and raised her arms above her head long enough to stretch her back. Her arms dropped like weights at her sides. Ten minutes later, his favorite part. In her short jogging shorts, a tight tank top, and her raven hair pulled back in a tight ponytail. She stretched her legs on the front porch, paying no attention to the things around her. Her only focus was on her mp3 player as she selected her music. Her favorite, guilty pleasure song, *It's Tricky* by Run DMC.

Her mp3 player was tucked in her bra. His hands started to sweat. If only he could be as close to her as that mp3 player was now. She started to run. From his vantage point, he could see her run a half mile down the road. At the half-mile corner, he moved his truck and continued to watch her. Down the big hill she would jog, slowing as she got down by the library. Beads of sweat would start to form on her face and chest. If only he had the chance to offer her a towel.

Finally she reached the local track where she would run around the inner lane once before heading back home. Up the hill. Her calves tightened. His heart raced. Would she make it up the hill today? He wanted to cheer when she made it to the top. Perfect in every way. Never failing. He remembered the days she struggled to make it up that hill. The many times she challenged herself to do better. With practice, this day had finally come. She made it to the top without slowing to a walk.

Back at the house, it was time to take a shower. He went to his usual place outside her bedroom window. He watched her in the mirror on her vanity as she gathered her things and went into the bathroom. Once he saw the steam from the shower, he raised his gloved hand and cracked the window. He sunk into the bushes, invisible to anyone going by and there he waited. It never took longer than five minutes.

The steam lurked through the bedroom and out the window. He breathed deeply her rose shampoo. If he could capture her scent in a bottle, he would keep it with him always. The water stopped running. Silent, he closed the window and secured himself in his truck once more. Someday, she would be Mrs. Bastian Clark. Someday, he would be with her, close enough that her smell would linger on his skin for days after.

*****

"How can this be so difficult? Explain it to me!" Allie shook her head and fell back in her chair. "Do not move evidence. Do not touch evidence. How hard is that to comprehend?"

"Well, that could be taken in a different way. I mean, what if they didn't know it was evidence?"

Allie stared at Carly. "If a man is murdered, whatever room he is in is evidence." The anger in her voice seemed to surprise her plucky sidekick but she didn't care. It wasn't rocket science. No thinking should be involved in deciding what was and wasn't evidence. "Whatever is in that room is evidence. If there is a picture crooked on the wall and you can see there's something behind it, you don't touch it!"

"Well, how could I have known that the picture was evidence?"

"Your first clue should have been the fact there was a *safe* behind it! The reason it was crooked on the wall was because someone had moved it to get to the safe." Allie slapped her desk and pointed a finger at Carly. "You're lucky your badge isn't getting taken away."

Carly merely shrugged. "My mom always told me that my perfectionism would be my downfall."

Allie took a deep breath in an attempt to

calm herself. It would be all right. A print could still be found. If this had been a rookie mistake she would have overlooked it but this wasn't the first time Carly had compromised evidence.

For someone who had worked with the police for so long, Carly should know better. Allie glanced over at Carly. The woman stood frowning and pushing all of the buttons on the copier. Suddenly she flashed a flirtatious smile as Marcus walked by. Allie groaned and buried her face in her hands. She needed to get out or she'd have to work on finding an alibi for Carly's murder.

All at once Marcus sped past her desk in his office chair. Allie struggled to hide her smile. Marcus would make a fool of himself to get a smile out of her. He came crawling back, one foot landing heavily in front of the other.

Allie tried to look as uninterested as possible.

"You smell nice. What is that? New shampoo?"

"Old shampoo. My mom makes it from her rose garden. We've discussed this. Do we have a case?"

Marcus smiled and handed her a cup of coffee. "Cheerful as always. I'm fine, by the way." He handed Allie a folder. "The brother-in-law's cousin or twin or step child…"

"It was the brother-in-law's nephew."

"Right, that guy. He confessed. Case closed."

Allie shook her head, leaning back in her chair to sip her coffee. They'd worked this case for two months. She'd almost given up. Together she and Marcus had closed numerous cases, but they'd had a losing streak recently.

"You sure you want to leave me? We make a great team." Marcus took a sip of his coffee and propped his feet up on the chair beside her desk.

"Yes, I want to leave." Allie heard Captain Ashton calling for them. "The sooner I get out of this town the better. Tell Ashton I'll be there in a minute. I'm just going to refill my coffee."

"All right, but hurry. Just because you're leaving next week doesn't mean you can slack off until then." Marcus winked at her and stood up. He pushed his chair over to his desk before strutting to Ashton's office.

It would be very hard to leave Marcus and everyone at the precinct, but she had to move on. Things were getting too difficult to stay. Allie opened her desk drawer to reveal a small box. She glanced around the precinct, relieved to see everyone was busy. She took a pair of scissors and slowly split the tape on the lid of the box. She peeled back the lid and swallowed hard, glancing around to ensure she was alone.

Biting her lip, she peered into the box, heart racing. Her breath caught in her throat. Teeth clenched, she reached into the box and pulled out several pink rose buds. Underneath them were the rest of the ingredients to make her mother's homemade shampoo. There was a typed note in the bottom. Allie pulled it out with a shaky hand. It read: Noticed you used the last of your shampoo this morning.

Allie dropped the note and roses back in the box and covered her face with her hands, her breathing labored. "Pull it together, Al."

A loud pounding sounded before Marcus hollered at her. "We don't have all day!"

She stood immediately, closing and locking her drawer. She slipped the key into her pocket; it weighed heavily against her leg.

Allie closed up the files on her desk. She hadn't found her secret admirer, but she'd found at least one more killer. She glanced at the details of the victim. This was one less case she had to put in her pile of shame; the unsolved pile. She didn't believe in the unsolved pile. Allowing murderers to escape was not a part of her job description. Failing wasn't an option. She'd found this killer, and she would find her admirer and put him where he belonged, behind bars.

2

"We just got this in. I want you *both* on it."
Ashton picked up a paper and handed it to him.

Marcus leaned forward to read the briefing.
"A prostitute?"

"Yep. You're wasting time."

Marcus pulled out his phone and sent a text
to a friend to get more information on the prostitute.
If anyone could give him information on their
victim, it was Kent.

Allie frowned at Ashton and opened her
mouth to argue. Marcus took his chance. "All right.
Come on Al. It's a bit cold out. You should get your
jacket. I'll get the car." Folding the paper he tucked
it in his back pocket. Marcus ushered Allie out the
door as quick as he could. He wouldn't let her start

another argument with the captain.

"Marc, why…"

"Shh." Marcus pulled Allie in the elevator with him. He held down the close door button, thankful the doors hid them from the watchful eyes at the precinct.

"Don't shush me, Marcus." Allie crossed her arms and glared at the floor. "You know, he's ridiculous for not letting me look into those cases. What could it hurt?"

"Not now, Al." The doors opened and the elevator chimed. Marcus smiled and nodded at the two women waiting. A glance at the floor number and he stepped back and made a sweeping motion with his arm. "Going down, ladies?"

"Don't mind if I do." One of them stepped in next to him, a little too close for comfort. He didn't have to look to know Allie was glaring at him. "Where are you off to, Officer?"

His phone chimed and he reached into his pocket to silence it. He turned his back on Allie, giving the women his full attention. "It's detective, actually, but you can call me Marcus."

The two women exchanged a glance then the taller of the two stepped closer, wrapping her long blonde hair around her finger. "So where are you off to, *Detective?*"

The doors opened and the elevator chimed. This was his stop. He smiled at the women. "Well..."

"A crime scene." Allie cut in. "We're late."

Marcus winked as he stepped out of the elevator. "Nice meeting you, ladies." Marcus sighed in contentment. "I think we're off to a good start.

And we're not late."

"I know but Barbie and her step cousin were on my every nerve."

Marcus laughed and pushed the button to unlock the doors. "Don't be jealous, Al. You know all you have to do is say the word and I'm all yours."

Marcus's seatbelt clicked and he handed her their new assignment. Allie snatched the paper from him and groaned. "I can't believe he stuck us with a prostitute case."

He skimmed over the text Kent sent him, thankful for his friends in low places. "Apparently she's a very good prostitute."

"How do *you* know?"

Marcus held up his phone wiggling it back and forth. "Kent."

"Who's Kent?"

"Friend of mine who works narcotics. He's gone undercover in that area before. Her name is Kathryn Thompson, goes by Katie." Marcus flipped on his blinker and turned toward Broadway.

Marcus pulled the car to a stop. Off to the side, away from the crowd were two young women. Prostitutes from the looks of it. Allie would want to talk to them. "Ready?"

"I'll meet you there."

Marcus nodded, leaving her to her own searching, and headed for the crime scene. "Be nice." He called over his shoulder, knowing it would get a rise out of her.

*****

Allie kept her eyes on the two women as she approached. They hadn't seen her yet or they were choosing to ignore her. "Morning ladies. I'm Detective Krenshaw. I just have a few questions for you." Allie flashed her badge, ready for any excuse the two would come up with. She was pleasantly surprised.

"Is it true that's Katie?"

"Yes, it's her." Allie had heard how prostitutes take care of each other on the streets. These women could help her piece together Katie's last moments. "How long has she been missing?"

The women looked at each other as if having a silent debate. Finally one made eye contact with her. "Since last night. She'd had a couple of jobs last night."

"When did you last see her?"

The woman cleared her throat, tossing her dark blonde cornrows over her shoulder. "On the street, maybe two blocks from here."

Allie nodded, noting the woman's reluctance. "What's your name?"

"You gonna write it down?"

"Not if you don't want me to."

Her chin went up a notch. "I'm Taffy." She motioned to the woman next to her. "Tray-C." Taffy's voice raised an octave on the last part of her friend's name. Allie ducked her head to hide her smile.

"Did she go with anyone?"

"Yeah. She went…"

"Taff, no." Tray-C elbowed Taffy and shook her head. "Daddy Cain won't like it." Tray-C looked down her nose at Allie. "We don't have to tell you nothing. You wanna talk, you talk to Daddy Cain. We done here." Grabbing Taffy's arm, the two swaggered down the street. Allie didn't miss

the way they both strained to catch a glimpse down

the alley as they walked by. There was real concern

in their eyes. The victim was their friend but for

fear of Daddy Cain they refused to talk.

Daddy Cain could be the killer.

Allie pushed through the crowd. She

showed her badge to the officer standing watch and

he lifted the crime scene tape for her to enter.

Marcus stood talking to the medical examiner.

Before she joined them, she went to see the body.

When she approached, the coroner's assistant lifted

the tarp to reveal the body. Her eyes grew large.

The prostitute had been shot and stabbed multiple

times in the torso, most of the damage being done to

her abdomen. This could be a type of hate crime;

someone lashing out at prostitutes.

"Thank you." She mumbled and the body was taken away in the coroner's van. Allie joined Marcus and the medical examiner. "Cause of death?"

"The obvious reason, shot to the head. The stabbing was done post-mortem." Dana Benedict was her favorite ME and she was glad to have her on the case.

"Did they say who found the body?" Allie glanced at Marcus.

"Anonymous call. They're trying to track him down now." Marcus held up an evidence bag with a gold cross necklace. "This was found on the body but I don't think it belongs to her."

"Why do you think that?"

"All of her other jewelry is silver and cheap. This is gold and real."

"Good point. Maybe we can track down the caller from the necklace." Allie sighed. "This is just too weird. Does this case seem familiar to either of you?"

Dana glanced at Marcus and shrugged. "Not really."

"Another gut feeling?" Marcus asked knowingly.

"Yes. I think this might be connected to our other case." Allie pulled out her phone and jotted down some quick notes. "Dana, keep me posted on what you find out."

Dana nodded, giving Marcus a shy smile before she got in her van.

"Really, Marc? You can't even keep it professional at a murder scene." Allie shook her head, exasperated.

"What did I do?" Marcus left the scene with her, ducking under the tape and pushing through the crowd.

Allie stopped as they got just outside the crowd. "She's here doing a job. You're here doing a job." Allie poked his chest for emphasis. "Keep your mind on the job and not on Dana's chest."

Marcus scoffed. "My mind *was* on my job. She's the one who gave me the phone number. I didn't ask for it."

Allie rolled her eyes, letting out a loud groan. "Forget it." She walked away from him, her head jerked side to side. "I need to just get over it. I have a playboy for a partner and there's nothing I can do about it." Allie pulled on the handle but the door didn't open. "Unlock the door, Marc."

The doors didn't unlock and she turned to

confront him, only to find him directly behind her. She looked up at him, his emerald eyes more serious than she'd ever seen them before. "I am *not* a playboy. You know me better than anyone. You know I'm not that guy."

"I'm sorry." Allie sighed and ran her fingers through her hair. "I'm frustrated and angry and sad. I feel like the bad guys are winning and there's nothing we can do to get ahead no matter how hard we fight." She licked her lips and looked back up at him. "I took my frustration out on you."

Marcus nodded and the car beeped as the doors unlocked. "The bad guys aren't going to win." He said simply and walked around the car, his mood seeming lighter. "You don't always have to take your frustration out on me, you know."

Allie climbed into the car. "It's your own

fault, you make an easy target." Allie shared a smile with her partner, glad they could move past the upset so quickly. They were a good team and Marcus was right. The bad guys weren't going to win.

*****

Shoulders tense. The man upset her. Why did she keep going back to him when all he did was upset her? Bastian shook his head. His fist slammed into the steering wheel. He would never upset her. Bastian's breath caught in his throat seeing how close Marcus was to her.

Jealousy boiled up inside him.

What did the man have that he lacked? He was twice the man Detective Marcus was and one day she'd see it. One day in the not so distant future.

<u>3</u>

Marcus could feel the tension in the room. Between Allie's frustration and the pressure from Ashton to solve the murdered prostitute's case, he was spent. It was sure to be a long night. A quick glance at his watch told him he needed to call Maddie. He stood up and slipped into his blazer.

"Al, I'm headed out for food. Pizza or Chinese?" Marcus knew she would pick Chinese but he needed her to stop thinking about the case for two seconds. If she didn't answer him, he would have to take her along.

"Chinese, please." Allie looked up at him, frowning. "I think I want sweet and sour chicken." She hesitated. "No wait, get me chicken fried rice."

"You always get chicken and you end up

eating my pork. Are you sure you don't want to reconsider? I might not share this time."

Allie groaned. "Fine, just surprise me."

Marcus pulled his cell phone out of his pocket and dialed Maddie as he got into the elevator. "Are you here yet?"

Maddie sighed through the phone. "I hate driving in the city. I can't find your street. I think I missed it."

"What street are you at now?" Marcus couldn't help but smile. Maddie was by far the most directionally challenged woman he'd ever known. She could get lost walking from her front room to her bathroom.

"Wait! I see it! I'm here! When are you coming home?"

"I don't think I will be. We have a case

that's going to keep us here all night."

"Then why did I come?"

"Because you missed me." Marcus smiled and slid into his car, clicking his seatbelt. "I'll be home eventually. I'll talk to Allie and see if we can have a late start tomorrow morning. I will take you out for breakfast."

"I can suffer with that."

Marcus heard the smile in her voice, glad she wasn't upset with him. "What a relief. I'm picking up Chinese for me and Allie. Do you want anything? I can drop it by for you."

"Um..." Marcus could hear her rummaging through something. "How long has this pizza been in here?" He heard her sniff.

"I got it a couple days ago. You're welcome to it."

"I'll eat that. You can take me out for Chinese later."

"How long will you be staying?" Marcus pulled alongside the curb and went into the Chinese restaurant he and Allie agreed was the best in town. He waved to the owner who came out to meet him.

"I can only stay the weekend. I plan on leaving Monday morning after you take me out for breakfast."

"Hold on a sec." Marcus shook hands with the owner. "How's business?"

"Better since you and Allie found us." His standard reply.

Marcus chuckled politely and told the man their order. He got back on the phone with Maddie. "You have high expectations. Breakfast twice in one weekend?"

"You can afford it. I'll see you tomorrow morning."

Marcus shook his head. He just might tell Allie he was leaving early so he could spend a little more quality time with his visitor.

*****

Allie groaned, rubbing her eyes in an attempt to stay awake. Marcus had been gone for what seemed like hours. Her stomach rumbled. How long did it take to drive three blocks?

A man cleared his throat and she glanced up at the precinct courier. He managed a small smile and presented her with a padded manila envelope. "A package arrived for you today. I must have overlooked it."

"Oh, thanks Sebastian. Do I need to sign anything?"

He pulled the clipboard from under his arm and gallantly presented it to her.

Allie managed a crooked smile and scribbled her name where indicated. "Thanks Sebastian. Have a good night."

He gave a quick nod and left, his back stiff.

As soon as she saw the typeset on the front of the package, her blood went cold. Her heart pounded against her chest. Not again. Turning the package over Allie stared at the carefully sealed envelope. She swallowed hard. It would be smart to have the package dusted for fingerprints. There was no time for that. Marcus would be back any minute. He could never find out.

Pulling the letter opener from her drawer, she slit the envelope open and dumped the contents on her desk. A single item fell out. Her heart dropped. An exact replica of the hairbrush she'd broken that morning. She hadn't even told Marcus. Allie dropped the envelope and it floated to the floor, landing beneath her desk. Her focus was on the brush.

She broke it in her bathroom. There were no windows. Part of her wanted to cry. He's back. It'd been two months since she'd received anything from him. Why couldn't she just be rid of him for good? The elevator door sounded and Allie swiped the brush into the top drawer. She stared at it a moment, still not believing it was starting over again. Marcus started across the room and she closed the drawer casually so not to draw attention to it.

"I hope you're hungry." Marcus set the bag of food on her desk.

"What took you so long?" Allie snapped. "Did you walk?"

Marcus frowned at her. "What happened while I was gone?"

"Nothing!" Allie swallowed hard. She had to calm down. Her ability to think outside the box made her a good detective. Reading people made Marcus good. She needed to keep herself in check. "What food did you get?"

"I told him to give me our usual but I think he gave me a whole lot of everything." Marcus started pulling out boxes of food. Allie snagged an eggroll from him and started stacking papers to the side. "Did you get our drinks?"

Allie shook her head. "Sorry, I forgot." Holding the eggroll in her mouth, she picked up a stack of files and moved them to a nearby chair.

"I'll go but since it's your turn to pay I'm dipping into your change jar." Marcus opened her desk drawer and Allie darted back to her desk and slammed the drawer, nearly crushing his hand. "Hey!"

"Sorry. Don't get in my change jar."

"You always pay out of your change jar." Marcus sat back, frowning as he observed his hand for damage. "What's gotten into you today?"

"I'm fine. I just don't want to pay out of my change jar. Here." Allie pulled a couple of crumpled dollar bills from her pocket and handed it to him. "I'll go find plates." Allie stayed by her desk until he left the room. She couldn't risk him coming back to look in the desk. Once he was out of sight, she opened the drawer and slid the hairbrush back into the padded envelope. She had a box of files she was taking home and on her way to the break room she slipped the envelope into the box. Wasting no time, she fetched the plates from the break room. She filled hers with fried rice and two egg rolls. Propping her feet up on a stack of files, she rested her plate in her lap and started reading the report Dana had sent her.

Would Dana be sending a file like this to Marcus about her? The stalker had been getting bolder, more personal. A shiver ran down her spine remembering his last gift. She'd meant to get milk on the way home but forgot. That night, her doorbell rang. On her front porch was a half-gallon of milk. Her exact brand. She couldn't drink regular cow's milk so she always bought almond milk. No one knew she bought almond milk. The note: You forgot to buy your milk.

"Orange soda, your usual."

The can let out a loud bang as it was put on her desk. Allie started. Her feet dropped to the floor causing her food to spill all over the floor. The file flew from her hands as her hand flew to her chest. "Marcus! You scared me!" She glanced back at him to find him frowning at the floor.

He scowled at her. "I scared you?" He bent over and swiped a can of soda from the floor. "What's bothering you?" He slammed the can down on the desk. His eyes sparked, losing the typical easy-going shine.

Her anger flared. He'd scared her. Why was he mad? Allie dropped her plate on her desk, a few pieces of rice falling from the plate. "Don't get hateful with me. You shouldn't be sneaking up on people."

"I wasn't!" He made a sweeping motion toward the door. "I was singing down the hallway! People three blocks away probably heard!"

"I doubt that. I never heard a thing. I was reading the ME report." Allie picked up the file. "It was scary." She winced at how weak and unconvincing the comment sounded even to her.

Marcus sighed, lowering himself into his chair. "I don't know what's bothering you Al, but you know you can talk to me about it." He looked back at her; the anger was gone, replaced with concern. "We good?"

Allie sighed and shook her head with a slight smile. "Of course." She reclaimed her seat, not bothering to clean up the mess on the floor just yet. She wanted to finish the ME's report. "Have you read this?"

"Not yet. I started reading it but I got bored."

Allie gave him a disapproving look over the file. Marcus just took a bite of egg roll and grinned. "Dana said there were two types of blood on Katie's face."

Marcus nodded and swallowed. "So what? Maybe Katie put up a fight. Then again, she was a prostitute. Maybe the blood got on her face before the actual killing. Maybe her client got angry."

"No, that's not it. There was no bruising or cuts on her. This is something else."

"What did your call girls at the crime scene have to tell you?"

"Gave me a little bit but said if I wanted to know more I needed to talk to Daddy Cain."

Marcus chuckled. "You talk to Daddy Cain.

Let me know how that goes for you."

Allie threw a fortune cookie at him. He caught it and wiggled his eyebrows before scooping the last of the rice on his plate into his mouth. "Who is that friend of yours? Ken?"

"Kent."

"Can you ask him about this Daddy Cain person?"

Marcus licked his fingers. "Yeah, but it'll cost ya."

"What do you want?"

"Your fortune cookie."

Allie tossed it to him. "You know I don't like them."

"Yes, but the question is why?" Marcus broke open the fortune cookie and smiled. "What do you know? 'You will meet the love of your life tonight.'" He handed the fortune to her. "Too bad we've already met. I felt we had real potential."

"Make the call." Allie laughed and threw the fortune on the desk. While Marcus called Kent, Allie finished reading the report. This whole case made no sense. From what she could tell, Katie died instantly from the shot to the head. Dana noted that the stabbing done to her torso was done post-mortem. Why would someone kill her then stab the body?

"Thanks man, I owe ya." Marcus hung up the phone and flapped the note in front of Allie. "The information you requested."

Allie took the paper and frowned. "This is just around the corner from the crime scene."

Marcus smiled. "I thought you would like that. Let's go talk to him."

"All right!" Allie stood up and folded the note in her pocket. Marcus grabbed her wrist to stop her. "What? Let's go."

"Tomorrow. I have a visitor in town."

"Who?"

"Maddie. I need to go home and see her. I haven't seen her in two months."

"Liar. You just saw her a couple of weeks ago for Thanksgiving."

Marcus shrugged. "Just the same. Stop being a workaholic." Marcus stood up and tossed the empty food containers in a plastic bag. "I'll even help you carry your stuff downstairs."

"There's still a lot of work to do."

"And it will still be here tomorrow."

"Someone's dead, Marcus." Allie held up her hand to stop his comment. "And they'll be dead tomorrow, but what about the killer. They might not be here tomorrow."

Marcus groaned and fell back in his chair. "Fine. What do you want me to do?"

Allie smiled. "Go home."

He perked up. "You mean it?"

"Yeah, go on and get out of here. Tell Maddie I said hi."

"Don't go anywhere tonight. We'll go talk to Daddy Cain tomorrow and I'll call Dana on my way home and have her check for DNA to see if we get a hit."

"That's perfect."

Marcus slipped into his coat. "What are you going to do tonight?"

"This case seems familiar to me. I'm going to search some old cases and see if there's a similar one. I'll send word to other precincts to see if they come up with anything."

"Don't stay here all night." Marcus picked up the bag of trash. "See you tomorrow. I'm taking Maddie out for breakfast. You can join us if you want."

"That's okay. I wouldn't want to take away from your time."

"She loves you, she wouldn't mind."

"Just the same." Allie typed up an email and sent it out to the other precincts before she shut down her computer and gathered her things to go home. Since Marcus went home there was no real reason for her to stay. She could do all her work at home. Her first order of business: adding the hairbrush to her collection.

*****

Bastian backed his truck into the drive and turned it off. He rested his head on the back of the seat. It had been a long day, but his last delivery had made it worthwhile. A smile came to his face as he closed his eyes, picturing her perfection once more. She'd been surprised by the hairbrush. He could tell she was pleased. She wouldn't even show it to Marcus. The man would have gotten upset that he hadn't thought to give her something so special.

Taking up his bag he got out of the truck and went in the house. He opened the door to the spare bedroom and flipped on the light. He smiled at the room's design. It was almost ready for her. He put his bag on the bed and pulled out a green rug. He unfolded it and placed it next to the bed. She liked getting out of bed and feeling the softness beneath her feet. She'd be coming to stay with him soon and he wanted her to be comfortable.

Biting his lip, he pulled a picture from his bag, then stepped back to observe his work. He compared the picture of her bedroom to his remodel. It was almost perfect. Two more items to complete the room. Bastian pulled a picture from his wallet and traced the edge of her face with his finger. In the picture she'd been scanning the crowd at a crime scene. He knew she was looking for him.

"Don't worry my dear, I'll get you soon." He pressed a kiss to her picture, picked up his bag, and left the room to make his supper. Five weeks until their anniversary. Best anniversary present ever.

4

Marcus stared at the menu, barely making out the words. Why was he up this early? Why had he stayed up so late? "What are you getting?"

"Omelet and chocolate milk." Maddie smiled. "Still not awake yet."

"Why did you keep me up so late? Old people aren't supposed to be up past nine."

"You're thirty-two. That's hardly old. And we weren't up that late. I mean, *you* weren't up that late. You fell asleep during the second movie."

Marcus smiled and leaned forward. "I work for a living. I'd been up since five."

"You knew I was coming. You should have taken a nap."

There was no winning. Marcus sat back and

focused on the menu. The waitress came over for their order. "I'll take the biggest, strongest cup of coffee you've got and bacon and eggs."

"That's adventurous." Maddie teased. "I'll have the Santa Fe omelet and a large chocolate milk please."

"All right, I'll go put your order in and be back with your drinks." The waitress looked at him and glanced away quickly when he made eye contact.

"How's Allie?"

Marcus looked at Maddie. "I don't know. She's been acting weird lately. She called me a playboy."

"No, you?" Maddie said in mock surprise.

Marcus pointed at her. "You know better…and so does she." Marcus shook his head.

"Let's talk about something else."

"Have you heard from Dad?"

"Really? Of all the things happening in the world, you choose to bring him up?" Marcus sat back and crossed his arms. Why did she have to bring him up? The man was good for nothing. He was a liar and a cheater. At the moment he was on the run from the government. If he had heard from him, he'd be finding him and arresting him.

"I guess that's a no. I just worry about him sometimes."

"There's no reason to. Anything he gets, he's had coming for a good long while."

"You know, what happened is in the past, Marc. You can't stay mad at him forever."

"Maddie, stop talking about it or I'm leaving."

Maddie sighed and linked her fingers together on the table in front of her. "All right, do you have a girlfriend?"

"Maybe." Marcus took out his wallet and handed her Dana's phone number. "I got this yesterday."

"Is it Allie's?" Maddie looked at him and wiggled her eyebrows.

"No, I've had hers for years." Marcus chose to ignore her teasing. She was really pushing his buttons today which could only mean she'd been in contact with their mother. "*This* is Dana's number."

"Dana? I know that name." Maddie winced. "I don't remember who she is though."

Marcus scoffed. "She's the medical examiner."

"That's right. I don't like her."

Marcus stared at her with large eyes. "What? I thought you liked her."

"No, she's too…" Maddie made a face. "Flirty. She's too flirty. You need a woman who can take care of herself." Maddie handed him back the number. "Like Allie for example. Why don't you just ask her to dinner or a movie?"

"She wouldn't see it as a date. The 'friend' category is a real thing and I'm in it." Marcus sat back when the waitress brought their drinks. If there was a way out of the friend category, he would have found it already. He'd been searching since he met Allie three years ago.

*****

"Allie, someone here to see you."

"Thanks Beth." Allie picked up her coffee and walked back toward her desk. A man sat at her desk with his back to her. Carly sat on the edge of the desk talking and giggling. Allie rolled her eyes and walked faster. Trapped by Carly. "Carly, don't you have some filing to do."

"Oh, yes, sorry." She shot off the desk and started to walk away then turned back and beamed at Allie's guest. "It was so very nice to meet you Nate."

"Carly." Allie glared at her until she disappeared. With a sigh she sat down. "Sorry about that." She came around her desk and stopped short. The man stood up, towering over her. His blue eyes smiling and pleasant. He was tanned, most likely from being outside, though his charcoal three piece suit made it appear he was a businessman.

Allie checked the time. It was ten to seven. She hadn't expected Daddy Cain to be on time to their meeting but she really hadn't expected him to look like this man!

"Good morning. Are you Detective Krenshaw?"

"I am." Allie shook his slightly calloused hand and again she had to wonder at this man. Daddy Cain didn't seem to her the working type, but his hands suggested otherwise. "I'm glad you're here. My partner hasn't made it in yet. I expect him anytime and we can start our meeting."

The man frowned at her and gave a single slow nod. "Your partner?" He sounded confused, but gave his shoulders a slight shrug and relaxed against the back of the chair.

"Can I get you anything to drink? There's coffee or soda and water."

"Oh, I'm fine, thank you." He sat back down

and crossed his legs, brushing a microscopic piece of dirt from his pants. The silence was unnerving but she was at a loss for words. The man finally spoke up. "Have we met before?"

"Um…no. I don't imagine so. Why do you ask?"

He shook his head and got quiet again. She could not get over the way he was dressed. She'd met people like Daddy Cain before, or at least she thought she had. This meeting gave her an entirely different look at pimps. She hated that she found him attractive. The minutes ticked by when Allie finally picked up her phone and sent Marcus a text.

Where are you? Allie sent the man a shy smile. "I texted him to see where he is. He's never late like this."

The man pursed his lips and nodded. "I'm

not in a hurry."

Allie's phone chimed and she quickly opened the message from Marcus. *I'm already here. Hurry any chance you get.* Allie frowned and read the message again. Allie shifted in her chair and glanced at the man across from her. She cleared her throat and forced a smile. "Did you have an appointment with us?"

"No. I just thought it would be better to talk to you in person rather than on the phone."

Allie winced. "I'm sorry. Who are you?"

The man chuckled and uncrossed his legs, leaning forward. "Who do you think I am?"

"Well obviously a very important person." Allie could appreciate that he found humor in the situation but she had a job to do. "However, I have a meeting that's more important and it was scheduled. Unless you can walk and talk, it'll have to wait."

"In that case, let's walk." He stood up and shouldered a messenger bag. "I have some information that might be useful to you."

"Fine." Allie took her gun, badge, and a notebook from her desk drawer and slipped into her jacket. "Elevator."

"Floor?"

"Basement." Allie stepped into the elevator and the man pushed the floor button. "What information do you think I want? Are you a reporter?"

"You're not a very good detective." He pulled a badge from his pocket and showed it to her. "Nate Harris. I work homicide."

"Oh!" Allie would apologize but it was too

late for that. She was busy and he didn't seem to mind. "What do you got?"

"Two separate homicides. Both shot execution style." Nate pulled two files from his bag and handed them to her. "Found in their homes. I know for sure these two are connected and from what I saw in your email, there are a lot of similarities."

Allie flipped through the files. The elevator stopped before she was ready. "What does your schedule look like today? I'd like to talk about what you've found here."

"I'll be in and out. I can leave you my number."

Allie closed the file and handed it back to him. She dug her cell phone out of her pocket and unlocked it. "Go ahead and put your number in."

Allie handed him the phone and glanced at her watch.

"Where are you headed? Is it for this case?" Nate asked, handing back her phone.

"I have a meeting with our victim's boss."

"Daddy Cain?"

Allie's head snapped up. "How do you know that name?"

"Carly told me." The corners of his mouth wavered as if he were holding back his smile. "Did you think I was Daddy Cain?"

Allie frowned. "I'm late. I'll call you later."

"I'm sitting on pins and needles."

Rolling her eyes, she moved to her car. She glanced down at her phone and smiled when she saw 'Daddy Cain' had been added to her group of contacts. At least the guy had a sense of humor. She slid into her car, shaking her head. Allie sent Marcus a text to let him know she was on her way and sped out of the parking garage. This meeting with Daddy Cain may help piece her puzzle together.

*****

Marcus gulped as the girls sat on either side of him. He never should have come in here without Allie. What had he been thinking? The girl on his left crossed her legs, her foot rubbing up his pant leg. Once more, he checked his watch. Leave it to Allie to be late. Marcus shifted his legs away from the woman. The movement only brought him closer to the other.

"Ladies, leave." A short Hispanic woman stood in front of him wearing a black leather vest with a matching leather mini skirt.

Once the two girls had left, Marcus allowed himself to relax. "Thank you. I'm here for business only."

"I know." The woman's mouth curled up in a smile. "You're Detective Marcus, right?" She asked and slid into the booth on his right.

"Seems I'm at a disadvantage. You know me, but I don't know you."

She laughed breathlessly, her long red fingernail curling under his chin. "You know me better than you think, handsome."

*****

The moment she saw the room she knew she was in the right place. A mixture of alcohol and smoke invaded her senses. Shallow breathing was her only chance of walking out sober. She stopped and looked for any sign of her partner. Marcus stood to the side and raised his chin a notch in greeting.

"I hope you don't have your alcohol abuse test after this."

Marcus smiled and shook his head. "My thoughts exactly. Daddy Cain is waiting back there."

Allie started for the door.

Marcus grabbed her arm and stopped her.

"Everything all right?"

"Daddy Cain is…well…let's just say not what you're expecting." Marcus winced and shrugged.

Allie's mind went back to Nate Harris. She was confident the real Daddy Cain couldn't be more surprising than Detective Harris. "Thanks Marc. Let's go." The door was opened for them by two men who chose their profession well. Allie had always considered Marcus tall at 6'4" but these men were taller and twice as wide.

"Detective Krenshaw. Come in."

Allie walked in ready for business, but stopped dead in her tracks. There were seven people in the tiny room. Two more guards even larger than the ones at the door stood on either side of a throne-like chair in the corner of the room. Three women in nothing more than lacy undergarments sat on pillows along the wall. A large, dark as night man sat reclining in the throne while a woman dressed in a short black skirt and heels stood directly on his right holding a pad of paper. Why was Marcus surprised by this? Too much drama? She'd known Daddy Cain would want to show off, and he was doing a marvelous job of it.

Marcus nudged her and Allie stepped forward. "Thank you for meeting with us."

The man in the chair looked her up and down slowly. "Thank you for suggesting a meeting. How can I help you?"

"We're here about Katie Thompson."

The man glanced at the woman to his right. She nodded once and he turned his attention back to Allie. "What do you want to know?"

"Is it true she worked for you?"

The man glanced at the woman and when she nodded, he replied. "Yes she did. Good girl, Katie was. Sorry to hear she's gone."

Allie looked up at Marcus. "Am I the only one seeing the charade here?"

"Nope. You caught on faster than I did."

"How long did she work here?" Allie took a

few steps forward.

"About four years."

Allie walked right up to the woman and the two guards pulled out their guns and leveled them at Allie's head. "Did you kill her, Daddy Cain?"

The woman's mouth slowly curled up into a smile. "Put the guns down." She was obeyed immediately. "You're good detective." She glanced at the man in the chair. "Get out of here Ty. Everyone leave us."

"Daddy Cain?"

"Or Kris, whichever you prefer." Kris went over and sat down, crossed her legs and folded her hands in her lap. "You're on Katie's case, right?"

"That's right."

"Have a seat. I heard you are very good at what you do and I'm sure you've heard I'm good at what I do." Kris raised a glass to her lips, took a drink, and glanced over her cup at Allie. "I'm sure you know that you're not the only one investigating. I can't have people targeting my girls."

"I understand that. I'm just asking you to keep me or Marcus informed."

The woman turned her attention to Marcus and looked him up and down, starting at his feet. "I could keep him informed." The corners of her mouth turned up in a flirtatious smile.

"Kris, focus. I need to know some things about Katie if I'm going to bring her killer to justice."

Kris turned her attention back to Allie. "You're right. What do you want to know?"

"Tell me about Katie."

Kris shrugged. "She was a good girl, not the

type of girl you typically see here. She didn't tell me much about her past but from what I could tell, she came from money. Her parents are important people but Katie was very independent. She wanted to make her own way in the world. She was attending the college, just working for me at night." Kris seemed proud to make the announcement and Allie made a note of it.

"What was she studying?"

"She was a big history buff. Loved reading. She was majoring in psychology but she was taking a lot of history classes on the side just because she enjoyed it."

Allie nodded and made a note of it. "Did she work anywhere else?"

"Yes. She had an internship. I'm not sure where."

Allie wrote down internship with a question mark then wrote down a single question: Why was she killed on the street like a prostitute? "Did Katie have any enemies?"

"We all have enemies down here. Why do you think I changed my name and hired Ty? It's dangerous down here. People get themselves killed all the time."

"So why are you so surprised Katie was killed?" Marcus asked leaning forward.

"Because my girls don't get killed. Everyone knows better than to mess with Daddy Cain's girls." She smiled proudly. "Any other questions?"

Allie glanced over at Marcus and he gave a single nod before sitting back in his chair. "Would you be able to give us the names of some of Katie's regulars?"

"Katie didn't really have regulars because her schedule was so different. She didn't work every night and the nights she did work she would only be on the street for a few hours. Men liked her, she was a hot commodity but her schooling was important and she was only doing this for the money."

"So no one comes to mind. Someone who would ask about Katie's schedule?"

Kris shook her head. "No."

She was holding back. What wasn't she telling them? Allie closed her notebook. "Is there anything else you think I need to know?"

"Detective Krenshaw, I'll find my girl's killer, go have a donut." Kris stood up and took her cup to the bar to refill it.

Marcus and Allie shared a smile before they both stood to leave. "Thank you for your time Daddy Cain."

"You're welcome. Now don't waste any more of it." Allie headed to the door and stopped when Kris called her name. "Just stay out of my way, Detective."

"You said you heard about me. You know I'll do what I want. Good day."

5

Two hours. For two hours they'd been pouring over four different case files and the tension in the room hadn't lessened. Allie was ready to send Marcus and Nate to the gym to fight it out. As soon as Nate had walked in, Marcus had changed. His normal carefree attitude had evaporated. There had to be some history between the two.

"I'm still not convinced, Al." Marcus dropped one of Nate's files on the desk. "I have no doubt that Harris' cases are connected with Wymer's, but I don't think ours is connected."

"Look at this!" Allie laid out all three open folders. "Three victims, all shot to death in their homes. Same caliber gun, execution style, scene wiped clean. This *is* a hit man!"

"I agree, but ours wasn't like that. Katie's case is different."

"The only difference is the stabbing and that could easily be explained."

"Then explain." Marcus sat back and crossed his arms over his chest.

"Maybe the killer was trying to hide evidence."

"Evidence of what? She was a prostitute!"

Allie bit her lip, her mind scrambling for theories. "I don't know, Marc. We've closed hundreds of cases together. You've trusted me with every other hunch." Allie leaned forward, her eyes locked with his. "Trust me now."

Marcus sighed, his head bobbed up and down. He calculated the risks, always looking before leaping. She was just the opposite, she'd run off a cliff before she realized it. It made them a good team.

"Fine. I need more evidence before I agree to take this theory to Ashton."

"Deal. Let's go get some food. I'm starved." Allie glanced at her watch. "It's nine o'clock!"

"Time flies when you're having fun." Nate smiled at her.

Marcus groaned and let his feet fall loudly on the hardwood floor. "On that note, I'll raid the vending machine down the hall. Maddie's still in town and I don't want to waste any more time here." He stood and sauntered down the hall.

Allie frowned after him. "Nate, I'll be back." Allie followed Marcus to the vending machines and stepped in front of him so he couldn't ignore her. "What's the matter with you?"

"Nothing. I want some food. Get out of the way."

"No you don't. You can't lie to me. I'm a walking lie detector." She watched him, waiting for the smile. She didn't have to wait long.

"I can't believe you still remember that." Marcus chuckled and slipped his hands in his pockets. "Everyone knows it though."

"Yep, and no one lies to me. Now please, tell me what's wrong. Why don't you like Nate?"

"He just…I don't know. He puts off this vibe like he's better than everyone else. What detective working the streets wears a three piece suit? I mean, come on."

Allie shrugged. "I think it's cute. Maybe he's trying to look professional."

"So you're saying I don't look

professional?"

Allie looked from his tennis shoes, to his tattered blue jeans, and his dark gray t-shirt. "No, not really. You look like you could work for Daddy Cain."

"What?" He exclaimed and pushed her aside. "Get out of my way. I'm taking my chocolate and going home. You can work with Mr. Tight Pants in there by yourself."

Allie laughed and went back to her desk. A package. Allie stopped short and stared at the golden rectangle envelope. Less than two weeks. She heard Marcus coming up behind her. Every part of her wanted to stay away. One of these times the gift might not be something simple. It could be dangerous.

The package could be from someone else.

But who would send a package so late? Allie took slow heavy steps to her desk and forced a smile for Nate. "A package for me?"

"Yeah, that delivery guy dropped it off. He said he had to go to the bathroom but he'd be back for your signature. Apparently I couldn't sign for it." Nate shrugged and continued reading and making notes on his file.

Allie sat down and glanced up to see where Marcus was. Someone had stopped him in the hallway. She could see him talking and laughing. Allie picked up the package and carefully peeled back the corner. She glanced inside and frowned at the metal object. What was this? She swallowed hard and carefully peeled back the rest of the envelope.

"Allie."

Allie jumped, her head snapping up to see who was talking to her. Bastian stood smiling at her, his clipboard gallantly presented in front of him. "Sebastian, you scared me!" Allie forced a smile and took the clipboard from him.

"Bastian. My name is Bastian." He said through gritted teeth.

"Right. Sorry. You're working late again tonight?"

He laughed without humor. "Every night it seems, but you are too."

"Yeah, part of the job." Allie handed him back the clipboard. "Thank you. I hope you get to go home soon."

"Oh, I have a long night ahead of me." Bastian smiled and rested a hand on her desk. "Have a good night, Allie. Don't work too late."

Allie peered into the envelope at the metal picture frame. A picture frame?

"What did you get?" Nate closed his folders and started stacking up papers.

"Nothing." Allie closed up the folder. "I need to go home."

"I'll drive you. I'm about ready to call it a night anyway."

Allie nodded. She wanted nothing more than to be alone but letting Nate take her home would be faster than waiting for a cab at this hour. Allie tucked the envelope into her messenger bag. It was a ten minute ride to her house, then it was time to get to work. Allie waved to Marcus as she and Nate went to the elevator. He was upset but she didn't want to talk. He'd ask too many questions.

*****

Why did she go home with him? What were they doing? Marcus fumed as he turned the corner. What did Nate have that he didn't? A three piece suit? Marcus scoffed. "I could buy a three piece suit." He mumbled. Taking a deep breath, he sighed and shook his head. He was being ridiculous. Allie was entitled to go on a date if she wanted to. After all, he was going on a date with Dana tomorrow night. It would be Allie's turn to be jealous. Would she be jealous?

Marcus pulled into his parking spot and put the car in park. He needed to get in a better mood. Maddie was upstairs and would probably be ready to watch a movie or something. He'd called before he left the precinct to let her know he was coming. She would probably have a bucket of popcorn waiting for him. He wanted nothing more than to be alone, which meant he was probably better off with Maddie there.

Before he could open the door it swung open. "It's about time you're home! Are you working tonight or playing?"

"Neither. I'm moaning." Marcus pushed the door shut and locked the deadbolt. "You're sort of a woman. Explain something to me."

"Bad day at work?"

"Just humor me, will you?" Marcus trudged across the room and fell back in his recliner. "Why do women like suits?"

Maddie shrugged. "I dunno. It's hot. It's no different than men preferring women in a dress."

"I don't prefer women in dresses."

"You mean you would give a woman in a pant suit a second glance? I don't think so."

Marcus winced. "Maybe not a pant suit but there's nothing wrong with jeans or slacks even. That's beside the point though." Marcus motioned to himself. "What I'm wearing now is supposedly unprofessional and makes me look like a bum."

"No it doesn't. It's just boring. If you walked into work wearing a three-piece suit, that would be turning heads. What tricks do you have up your sleeve? Where are you headed? You could take a girl out to a nice restaurant and look presentable doing it."

"Really? You get all of that from a suit? What do you get from me right now?"

Maddie lowered her voice to sound more masculine as she mocked him. "Hey babe, you wanna go to a drive thru. I can afford the dollar menu."

Tired as he was, he couldn't let her get away with that. Marcus tackled her on the couch, grabbing her foot. "Apologize!"

"Never!" Maddie laughed, kicking her feet and screaming.

Marcus tickled her foot, dodging her kicks to avoid a black eye. He paused. "Apologize!"

"Okay, okay! I'm sorry! I'm sorry!"

Marcus dropped her foot and crawled off the couch. "Yeah, you'd better be sorry. You know I wouldn't take a date to a drive-thru."

Maddie was still giggling as she lay there on the couch. "You and Allie get in another argument?"

"No. It was a discussion."

"Who's the suit?"

Marcus flopped back into his recliner and

pulled his feet up. "A new detective friend of Allie's. Nate Harris."

"Jealous?"

Marcus glared at her. "I'm not jealous. I just don't get it. What does he have that I don't?" Marcus sighed and lay back, staring at the ceiling.

"Well, a suit for one thing."

He could hear the smile in her voice. He took the blanket from the back of his chair and threw it at her. "Go home. You're not welcome here anymore."

Maddie laughed and sat up. "Yes I am. Have you eaten supper?"

"No. What are you making me?"

"Pizza. I got one delivered."

Marcus reached in his back pocket and pulled out his wallet. He pulled out thirty dollars and handed it to her. "Here, go ahead and pay with this. I'm gonna take a nap." Marcus closed his eyes and settled into his chair. He heard Maddie in the kitchen singing as she took plates from the cabinet. He needed to stop complaining to her. She didn't come to hear him complain. The new year was coming. Maybe that should be his new year's resolution. No pity parties.

*****

Allie leaned against the door and sighed. Nate was such a nice guy, a gentleman. A smile teased the corners of her lips once more as she recalled the slow stroll up her walkway. Nate had stepped on the edge of the walk and fallen over in the dirt. Perfectionist that he was, he'd been brushing the dirt off his clothes for the whole ten minutes they'd talked on her front step.

She pushed against the door and tossed her bag on the kitchen table before going to the cabinet to get a glass. Nate had cheered her up considerably. The case had been weighing heavily on her mind. Rarely did one of her cases go unsolved for more than five days. Today marked day four and they were no closer to closing it. Waiting was the hardest part. Allie tugged open the refrigerator. A blue carton caught her eye.

Almond Milk. The smile fell from her face and she glanced behind her at the bag on her table. Closing the refrigerator, she set her glass down and took the envelope from her bag. Pursing her lips together she dumped the contents onto the table. A black picture frame, most likely purchased at a dollar store; harmless. The picture inside the frame; deadly. She rubbed her arms, willing the goose bumps to leave.

The picture was of her. She was leaning against a charcoal SUV; the charcoal SUV Marcus had sold over a year ago. Judging by her haircut, this picture had been taken almost two years ago. She'd been staring straight into the camera when the picture was taken. She'd seen him.

Her breathing became labored. Allie stepped back and rested her hands on her knees. Her stomach churned. He'd been close to her, so close. What else did he know? What else had he seen? Tears threatened. Her heart hammered in her chest. She had always been proud that she could control her fear. At this moment there was no controlling it. Her breath came sharp and fast. She had to calm herself. One look at the picture sent her spiraling.

Her head was spinning, her stomach uneasy.

She had to gain control. Allie sat down on the floor, pulling her knees to her chest. She reached a shaky hand into her pocket and pulled out her cell phone. Marcus. Allie listened as the phone rang in her ear slow and rhythmic. Voicemail. Allie ended the call and fought the tears that threatened. She needed someone. Where was Marcus?

A knock sounded on the door. Allie gasped and bit her lip, burying her face in her hands. Who was at her door? What did they want? Was it him? With trembling hands, she pulled her gun from the holster on her hip. On her hands and knees she crawled to the edge of the kitchen and peered around the corner.

"Oh Allie, what are you doing?" She whispered quietly. "You're a cop. You've got a gun. You're in control." Taking a few deep, shaky breaths, she pulled herself to her feet. With her gun in hand, close to her side, she took a few cautious steps toward the door. The knock sounded again. "Who is it?" She called.

"It's me."

Nate. Allie sighed with relief. She opened the door and stared at him as tears pooled in her eyes.

He stood smiling, a pair of handcuffs dangling from his finger. "I think you dropped these. They're not…" The smile fell from his face when he saw her. "Allie, what's wrong?" He stepped inside and closed the door. "You're shaking like a leaf. Come sit down." Nate put his arm around her shoulders and ushered her to the couch. "Why do you have a gun? Give me that." Nate easily took the gun from her hands and set it down on the floor next to the couch.

Allie buried her face in his shoulder, her tears couldn't be contained. Nate's arms held her securely. She felt safe. How long had it been since she'd felt this safe?

<u>6</u>

Marcus kept his head down when he heard Allie come into the room. She laughed. Nate must be with her. Not only was he the guy in the suit, now he was the funny guy in the suit. Carly came by and handed him a report.

"This just came in. I thought you might like to read it and give it to Allie."

"Why aren't you giving it to her?"

"She's with Nate. She doesn't want to be bothered."

Marcus took a calming breath and thanked Carly. He frowned at the report. An anonymous tip had brought the police to the alley where they'd found Katie. Who was the anonymous tipper? Why were they anonymous? Marcus looked at the number the call came from. He had a friend who could track down that number for him.

He reached for the phone and dialed his friend. "Scott? Marcus. Run a number for me, will ya?"

"Sure. I'm a little backlogged right now. Text me the number and I'll let you know what I find."

"I'll be waiting." Marcus hung up, sent the text, and then gathered up his papers. He passed Allie's desk, hoping to go unnoticed.

"Where you going? Did you find something?" Allie stopped him dead in his tracks.

Taking a steadying breath he turned on his heel and forced a smile. "Just going back to the crime scene. A few things aren't adding up for me."

"Which crime scene?" The sound of his voice made Marcus cringe. However one look at the man's face told him he was genuinely curious and focused.

"Katie's. Have either of you gotten information on the anonymous caller?"

"Zilch." Nate glanced at Allie. "You?"

Allie shook her head, frowning. "What else is the crime scene going to tell you? We searched the whole place. The only thing of significance anyone found was that gold cross. I thought you were running this hit man case with me. I thought we'd agreed."

"We did, but that doesn't mean this anonymous caller didn't see our hit man. He could have been a witness to whatever happened. This caller could *be* the hit man!"

Allie weighed what he was saying. He saw the moment she agreed with him. "Fine. We'll come with you."

"No!" Marcus winced at how desperate he sounded. "I mean, no. You and Nate stay here, find connections. Finish putting the board together. It'll be fine." A jazz melody could be heard faintly. Marcus blew out a sigh and reached into his pocket. "That'll be Scott for me. Really, you do this." He took several slow steps backwards as he pulled out his cell phone and answered. "Scott, that was quick." Marcus turned and rushed to the elevator.

*****

"I thought you said you got along with your partner." Nate hung a picture of the gold cross up on the board.

"We do."

"Seems like he's avoiding you."

"No, he's avoiding you." Allie put her hands on her hips and frowned at him. "Do you know Marcus? I mean did you know him before this case?"

"I don't think so, no." Nate's brow furrowed. "What's his last name?"

"Marcus." Allie bit back a smile. "It's his first name that he won't tell anyone. If you find it let me know."

"Wait, *you* don't even know his first name?"

Allie shook her head. "He was already here when we became partners so I never got the chance. Ashton says he is sworn to secrecy and he won't tell. Apparently anyone who knows Marcus' first name has been threatened or bribed not to spill the beans."

"Hm, that's interesting, a case to solve with great reward." The corner of Nate's mouth hitched up in a smile.

She couldn't help but stare at his lips. After their emotional encounter the night before, she couldn't stop thinking about kissing him. Allie averted her eyes and started straightening some files on her desk. "So did you say something to him?"

"To who?"

Allie sighed. "To Marcus!"

"Like what?"

"I don't know; something to make him mad?"

"I've hardly said two words to the man." His shoulders were tense; his hand gestures suggested he didn't like the questioning. "The only time I've talked to him has been right here with you."

Allie leaned against her desk and crossed her arms over her chest, her eyes on the murder board. Why didn't Marcus like Nate? Allie glanced at Nate out of the corner of her eye. Marcus had told her he didn't like the suit. She liked the suit. Everything about Nate was inches from perfection. There was never a hair out of place, clean shaven, sparkling white teeth, ocean blue eyes you could drown in and the suit. She'd seen him in a three piece suit, a plain black suit and tie, a suit with no tie. The man knew how to dress, there was no mistaking that.

Her phone rang, interrupting her thoughts, making her realize she'd been gawking. *Focus, Allie.* She pulled out her phone and smiled. Marcus. "Hey Marc, find anything interesting that you're going to share or were you planning on keeping that to yourself as well."

"Stop it." Loud music played in the background and she could hear people screaming and cheering.

"Where are you?"

"I think I found something but I need you to look at that necklace. Is there an engraving on it or anything?"

Allie pulled the picture off their board and squinted at it. "Not that I can tell from the picture. Let me look at the actual piece. Can I call you back?"

"Um…yeah. That should be fine. If I don't answer leave me a message and let me know." Marcus gasped followed by a crash and loud laughing and cheering.

"Where are you?"

"Not now. Just call me back when you get the information."

The phone beeped in her ear. He hung up. Allie looked at Nate. "Did that cross necklace say anything? Was it engraved?"

"There were some flowers on it."

So there had been an engraving, it just wasn't showing well on their picture. Or Carly took a picture of the backside of it. Allie looked over at Carly. The girl bouncing up and down, bobbing her head as she filed and listened to her iPod. Rolling her eyes, Allie went over and slammed her hand down on the table. Carly jumped and jerked the head phones from her ears.

"I need you to go find that cross necklace we got in. Marcus needs it."

"It hasn't come back from the lab yet."

Allie nodded. "Fine. What are you doing?"

"Filing. Listening to the radio." Carly smiled.

"Get busy. There's still a lot left to do." Allie went to her desk and slipped her coat on. "The lab has that necklace. I need it. Want to come with me?"

"Definitely. Let me get my coat. I hung it in the break room."

Of course he did. Allie bit her lip, watching him hurry off to the break room. He took his coat and slipped into it with ease. He fastened the buttons and donned his scarf. Still she couldn't believe this man's fashion sense. She'd never known a man to dress like that and work homicides.

*****

Allie had been spending too much time with

Nate Harris. He didn't like it. The man didn't like it.

Why couldn't she see that he was all wrong for her?

Bastian's hands clenched the steering wheel. He

needed to talk to her. Needed to warn her. Nate was

bad news. Would she listen to him? He had to try.

Bastian jerked the truck door open. He'd just slid to

the ground when his phone rang. He looked at the

phone, then back at Nate and Allie.

He let out a groan and swiped the phone off

the seat. "Bastian."

"Bastian, you forgot one of your deliveries. I

got a call from a Lucinda Perkins. She lives on

Richmond. Do you have that package?"

Bastian scrambled back into the truck and

scanned the few boxes he had left to deliver. "What

is it? A box? Envelope?"

"She's expecting a box."

Of course it would be the last box he looked at. "I've got it Simon. I didn't see it. I'll take it over to her."

"Do it now."

"I'm on the other side of town."

"Do it now. It should have been delivered already."

Bastian clenched his teeth. "If she would wait longer then not everyone's packages would be late."

"She's the mayor's daughter. She isn't going to wait. Deliver the package now or I'll have to write you up for insubordination."

"Fine." Bastian hung up and threw the phone on the dash. He glanced up once more to see if Allie had come back out of the building. No sign of her. He'd hoped for one last glimpse. He turned the key in the ignition and the truck roared to life. He would be busy for the rest of the day. He wouldn't be able to see Allie.

Bastian picked up the envelope on his dash and smiled. He could at least leave her present for her. At least she would know he hadn't forgotten her. They would still be together. Two weeks.

*****

Marcus answered the phone on the first ring. "Allie, what did you find?"

"There's an engraving here. It's *P. Hanson.* That's it."

Marcus groaned and rubbed the back of his neck. "Great, another dead end. When will we catch a break with this case?"

"Well hold on. There was a fingerprint they were able to lift. They're running it now but I doubt they'll find anything."

"Thanks Al." Marcus hung up and set his phone on the table. He glanced across the table to Dana. "Nothing. The necklace had *P. Hanson* engraved on it but that won't get us anywhere. They're running a print but Allie doesn't have much hope."

Dana shrugged. "Something will turn up, it always does. Did you ask Carly about her progress with Scott's tip?"

"I should probably call her." Marcus picked up his phone with renewed hope. Carly had been eager to help him. She would work hard to prove herself.

"Hi Marc." Carly answered cheerfully.

"Find anything?" Marcus resisted the urge to cross his fingers.

"Nada. However, the DNA on the necklace was a match."

"What DNA?"

"They didn't call you. They called me. I was the one who requested it. I was the one who thought of it so why shouldn't they call me? No one thought the necklace was important, but I did. I also told you whose necklace it was, but you wouldn't believe me on that one either."

Marcus took a calming breath. "Come on, Carly, what did they find?"

"Polly Hanson. The other DNA on the necklace didn't find a match."

"Tell me you ran her name."

"I did. She's dead."

"Another victim?"

"No, she died a few months ago. I remember

that story being in the papers. I told Allie this the other night. It was tragic. Polly and her husband were just leaving their wedding. Her veil blew off and she was running to catch it, got hit by a kid riding his bike. She fell down, hit her head and died. She had an aneurism that ruptured. So sad."

Marcus frowned. "She was killed three months ago?"

"Yes, DOD is September 21st."

"Katie was killed on the 21st. What's the husband's name?"

"Willard Gates."

"Thanks, I gotta go." Marcus hung up and dialed Allie. "Al, I need the dates of the murders."

"All of them?"

"Yes." Marcus pulled a pen and notebook from his back pocket. Allie read off the dates.

Frustration set in. "All right, never mind. I think I found our anonymous caller. I'm going to go talk to him."

"Good! I'll come with you!"

Marcus heard her chair scrape on the floor. She was anxious. "All right, I'll come get you. Are you at the precinct?" Marcus put his phone down at his side and kissed Dana on the cheek. "I gotta go. I'll see you tonight? Still on for our date?"

"Definitely. Pick me up?"

"Seven sharp at your apartment."

"See you then."

Marcus got back on the phone. "Are you ready?"

7

Allie came around the corner and stopped short. Nate was sitting at her desk frowning at a picture frame. Her mind scrambled. What picture was he looking at? Her stalker had sent her six pictures. She'd been looking at her collection before she'd come to work today. All of the pictures had been there. Had he sent her another gift?

She tried to walk at a normal pace, but ended up scrambling to her desk and jerking the picture frame from his hand. "What are you doing?" She turned the picture around and breathed a sigh of relief. The picture was of her, Marcus, and her two college friends when they'd gone to the top of the empire state building last year.

"I was just looking. It fell over."

Allie nodded. "Sorry, I guess I'm just a little on edge."

Nate smiled. "Much like you were the other night. You still haven't told me what that was all about."

"Can't a girl have a nervous breakdown?" Allie smiled and stood the picture back up on her desk. She missed Lindsey and Tory. They needed to plan another get together soon. Allie opened her drawer for her gun, but found a manila envelope instead. Typewriter font. A chill crawled down her spine. It'd only been four days.

"Everything all right? Isn't Marcus coming to get you?"

Allie slammed the drawer shut. "Yes, of course. I was just getting my gun." Allie stood up and started for the door. Nate caught her arm and she jerked around to face him.

"You didn't get your gun." Nate chuckled and easily reached across the desk to get it for her. He pulled the manila envelope from her drawer. "Apparently you got this too."

Allie stared at it, making no move to take it from him. "Put that back."

"What is it?"

"I don't know."

Nate rested a hand lightly on her shoulder. "Allie, you're white as a sheet. What's wrong?"

Tears threatened. At this point Nate would never want to date her. She'd done nothing but cry every time he came around. "I don't like to get packages."

"So much it makes you cry? And who doesn't like to get packages? I thought everyone liked it."

"Well I don't!" She snapped and wrapped her arms around her middle. "Put it back."

"Can I open it?" Before she could answer, he ripped the envelope open and dumped the contents on the desk.

"Nate!" Allie frowned at what fell on the desk. "What is that?" She took the small white square by the corner and flipped it over. Whatever was on the other side was heavy. A sticker? A large felt letter?

"A?" Nate frowned. "What does that mean?" Allie said nothing so he continued. "A red A. Like the scarlet letter. Are you married?"

Allie shook her head, her eyes glued on the letter.

He chuckled. "Let me guess, some friend of

yours has a sense of humor."

Allie's head wagged from side to side. "Not exactly."

"Allie, what is it?"

"Put it back. I need to go. Marc will be waiting." Allie reached into her desk drawer for her gun. With the Glock on her hip, she felt somewhat safer.

"Hold on. You're going to tell me what this is all about. Sit down." Nate stared her down, his eyes challenging her.

Allie calculated how far it would be to the stair door. She was a fast runner, but was he faster? *Why are you fighting Allie? What could it hurt to tell him?* "All right fine." Allie sat down, stealing a final glance at the elevator. She could tell Nate. He could handle it. Marcus couldn't. Marcus would be on a mission to find this guy and take care of him. Nate seemed like he would follow her lead.

"First, who sent you this?"

Allie swallowed hard. "I don't know."

He looked skeptical. "You don't know."

"Nope."

"All right, fine. Did they send you something the other night when I dropped you off?"

"Yes."

"Is that why you decided to call it a night?"

"Yes."

Nate sighed and leaned forward, linking his fingers together in front of him. "Come on, Allie. You can trust me."

Allie glanced at the elevator, then her phone. What if Marcus came in and overheard? "Marcus can't know about this."

"We're not exactly best friends." He said dryly.

"Good point." Allie took a deep breath and blew it out. "I…" She hesitated and glanced around, leaning forward her face inches from his. "Almost three years ago I started receiving these gifts. The first gift, it was like a child sent it. A single rose. It said it was from my secret admirer. Harmless right?"

"So far. Go on."

"Well, since then the gifts have gotten more personal, downright creepy. I'm slightly lactose intolerant. I can have some dairy products but I really shouldn't. I drink almond milk. I come home from work one day and there's a cooler on my front porch with a carton of almond milk inside. The note said that I forgot to get milk." Allie watched his eyes to gauge any reaction. His eyes stared intensely, emotionless.

"What happened the other night?"

"It was a picture of me, taken two years ago in Marcus's old car."

"Why did that make you break down?"

"His reflection could be seen in the car and I was looking right at him. How can I not know who he is? The picture reminded me of some of the other pictures he's sent me. They're mostly pictures of his arms, chest, and etcetera. My bed was in the background of one of the pictures. He bought me flowers and said he liked my shampoo and I should make some more. Nate, it's getting more and more personal and I don't know what to do."

Nate nodded and held up the scarlet letter. "What is the significance of this?"

Allie shook her head. "I don't know." She opened the manila envelope and shook her head. "No note."

"What kinds of things has he said to you?"

"Just a bunch of talk about how much he loves me and admires me. He says what he likes about me, takes pictures of himself. You can tell he's been working out, trying to impress me I guess?" Allie sighed and ran her hand through her hair. "It's changed my entire life. I never wanted it to, but it can't be helped."

"Why don't you tell Marcus about this? He could help you find this guy."

"I know, but Marc can get a little overprotective. I don't want him to worry. This guy seems to be staying back; I don't think he would hurt me if I met him."

"Or he's crazy and will over-react at the smallest thing you do that he doesn't like. Allie, you could change your hair color and it could make him mad enough to want to kill you."

"He won't hurt me. I'm confident of that."

Nate huffed out a sigh and held his hands out. "All right, what can I do?"

"Don't tell Marcus."

"Yes, we've covered that."

The elevator door chimed and Allie glanced that way to see Marcus looking impatient. She smiled and looked back at Nate. "Are you coming?"

"No, I've got an assignment I need to work on. I'll catch up with you later."

Allie smiled and kissed his cheek. "Thanks for listening." Allie moved to the elevator Marcus was holding for her. "Who is this guy?"

A hand stuck between the elevator doors just before they closed. The doors opened once more and Bastian stepped into the elevator with them. He nodded at Marcus. "Detective." He smiled at Allie. "Good afternoon. Did you get your package?"

"I did thanks." The doors closed once more and they started their descent. "Who are we going to see, Marc?"

"You've let your guard down."

Allie shrugged, unable to stop smiling. "He's sweet." Allie glanced at Marcus out of the corner of her eye. "He *listens* to me when I have a hunch."

Marcus's mouth dropped open and he turned to gawk at her. "Really? *He* listens?"

Allie laughed. "Marc, you make this too easy." The elevator chimed at the first floor and they stepped out. Bastian held the door for them as they exited onto the street. "Have a good day, Sebastian." Allie raised her hand and followed Marcus to his car.

"You do know his name is Bastian."

Allie winced. "I'm terrible with names, you know that."

"You remembered Nate's well enough." He mumbled and unlocked the car.

"You're jealous!"

"No I'm not because in a couple of weeks, after we've solved this case, he'll be gone."

"Unless we start dating."

"You won't."

Marcus seemed confident of the fact. Allie got in the car and put on her seatbelt. "You seem pretty sure of yourself, Marc. He likes me. I like him. Why wouldn't we give dating a try?"

"You're too sensitive."

"No I'm not!"

Marcus looked skeptical. "You are Al. You take things personally that shouldn't be. You get your feelings hurt all the time but because you're supposed to be this tough no nonsense cop, you put on a face. Anyone who gets close to seeing the real you, you run." Marcus pulled into traffic and headed for the highway.

Allie couldn't deny it. "I've let you stick around."

"Holding me at arm's length for the last three years doesn't count." Marcus handed her a file. "Carly is meeting us there. She found him so I told her she could come along."

"Carly, did?" Unbelievable. Why did he ask

Carly for help? Why wasn't he asking her?

"If you'd give her a chance, she's pretty good."

"Of course. She quickly obeys your every command because you'll smile at her if she does well. Despicable." Allie skimmed the file. "So he kept his new wife's cross necklace. That ended up in the alley. He's our caller?"

"It's possible." Marcus slowed, straining to see the house numbers. "There it is. And there's Carly's Jeep. Be nice to her, I mean it."

"As long as she doesn't talk to me." Allie forced a smile and got out of the car. She stared up at the big house. This was it.

*****

What was she doing? Bastian marched up the steps to the attic and slammed the door. How could she do this to him? How could she do it to them? She was impatient. Lonely. He understood that. He was lonely at times too. Bastian stopped and stared out the window. Maybe kissing the suit had been her way of showing him how impatient she was getting. Angry as it made him, he couldn't hate her for it.

The new suit had no excuses. He shouldn't be getting so comfortable with Allie. He wasn't good for her. Bastian sent the letter as a sign that Allie was already taken, but the suit didn't care. He had to be stopped. Bastian went over to the closet and opened the door. He stopped short when he saw the dress. His jaw clenched. Carefully, he pulled the clothes back and lightly fingered the feather-light material of the lavender gown. She'd been a vision in it.

Bastian forced the thought from his mind. She was gone. Rejected. He had Allie now. He'd never be alone again. Bastian took a box from the closet shelf and carried it downstairs. He'd bought the gun for protection years ago and vowed to only use it for protection. Allie was his, he had to protect her.

*****

Willard Gates was by no means a menacing sort of man. A bit odd, but he seemed likeable. Willard worked hard and was taking care of himself, even if he was living with his parents. Simple and clumsy.

Willard stood staunch at the front of the grocery store accepting the verbal assault from an irate customer. Everyone in the store was pretending to ignore the angry woman but there was no denying she had everyone's attention. Nate slipped his hands in his pocket and rubbed his badge, tempted to pull it out and escort the woman from the building.

The woman finally left with a discount in hand and Willard went up the stairs to his office. Nate jogged up the stairs and glanced down at the busy check-out lines. The store wasn't Fort Knox but no one questioned him. He stepped into a long hallway. There were four doors. Only one had a name and it wasn't the name he was looking for.

He straightened his suit and tie, ran his hand through his hair, and rapped on the door twice. Someone inside beckoned him to come in. A man sat at the desk, not even bothering to look up. Not Willard.

"Be with you in a minute."

He pulled the badge from his suit coat pocket. "Detective Nate Harris. I'm with the police. I'm looking for Willard Gates."

The man groaned. "I said just a minute."

He rolled his eyes and left the office. Could grocery store work really be that important and mind boggling that he couldn't be disturbed? Doubtful. Nate closed the door behind him, pocketed the badge, and went to the next office. He rapped twice on the door, no answer. He tried the knob. Locked. He moved on. "Third time's the charm." He mumbled and rapped twice.

"Who is it?"

"Police. I need to speak with Willard Gates."

The door opened a crack and Willard stared at him with large eyes. "How did you find me?"

"It's what I do." Nate stuck his badge in Willard's face. "Detective Nate Harris. I need a few minutes of your time." Willard opened the door wide and stepped back. Nate pocketed his badge. "I need to talk to you about the call you made the other night."

Willard winced, rubbing his hands together. "I know, I know, I should've done something. I'm sorry. I just couldn't help her."

"I know. That's not why I'm here. I need to know what you saw that night."

Willard bustled over to his desk and started jerking open his desk drawers. "I-I-I don't know what you mean."

"It *was* you that called about the dead woman?" Nate unbuttoned his suit coat and sat down in the chair across from Willard's desk, taking in his surroundings.

"Y-y-yes tha-that was m-me."

"So then you *were* there that night." He sat back in his chair, brushing some dust from his pants. One thing was for certain, Willard was no housekeeper. A few minutes in the room and he was ready to go home and shower. *Focus. Five minutes and you can breathe the free air again.*

"I didn't kill her!"

"I know that."

"You do?"

"It's obvious you didn't do it." This small, insignificant man couldn't kill an ant. If he did he would die of remorse. He didn't have the guts to kill another human being. "Tell me what you saw that night."

Willard pulled a medicine bottle from his

desk drawer. "Anxiety." He explained. His shaky hands could hardly keep hold of the pills, let alone put them in his shaking mouth. He took a swig of the bottled water. "Sorry. What did you ask me?"

Nate sighed and folded his hands in his lap. Was it even worth questioning this man? "Mr. Gates, either tell me what I need to know or I'll have to take you into custody for obstruction of justice."

"You can't do that. Can you?"

"Withholding information in an ongoing investigation is a criminal act, Mr. Gates. I need information."

"Fine. Fine." He sighed and sat down at his desk rubbing his face in his hands. "It was awful. Just awful."

"Details. Everything you can remember."

"I was lonely. I'm not the kind of guy that goes to places like…like that. It's distasteful and un-Christian."

"Yet you were there. Go on."

Willard shrugged. "I missed Polly. I thought of dating again but it's so hard for a guy like me, you know?"

The man was trying his patience. "I'm sure it is."

"I had some money that Polly and I had planned to use on our honeymoon so I went down there, just to see. I was really nervous. I met that girl. Katie. Oh, she was real pretty." Willard stopped to clarify. "She wasn't as pretty as my Polly."

"I'm sure. Go on." There would be a much faster way to get the information but now wasn't the time for that. Maybe soon he could switch tactics.

"The man came out of nowhere. He was tall. Six foot maybe? Taller than me. It was dark. He was wearing a black suit, black shirt, black tie, black gloves." Willard raised shaking hands to cover his face. "And then..." Willard whimpered.

"Then what, Mr. Gates?"

Willard sighed and dropped his hands, suddenly calm. "He shot her. Right in the head." His face scrunched up as if he were about to cry. "It went everywhere. The blood. I'll never forget. She just dropped to the ground. I stared at her then looked up at the man. His eyes."

Nate stood up and leaned against Willard's desk, unable to stop the smile that graced his face. "What about his eyes, Mr. Gates?" Nate asked in a hushed tone.

"They were blue. Light blue but brown around the pupil." Willard's eyes raised and locked with his. Willard gasped. "No."

"Hello Mr. Gates." Nate pulled his gun from its cradle. "I don't like collateral damage."

"Please! I haven't told anyone. I *won't* tell anyone, I swear!"

Nate twisted the silencer on the end of his gun as he walked around the desk. "Oh, I know you won't, Mr. Gates. I'm truly sorry. You were just in the wrong place at the wrong time." Nate put the gun to the back of Willard's head.

"My mother. What about my mother? What will she do?"

"You should've gotten life insurance."

<u>8</u>

Allie flashed her badge asking for Willard Gates. The cashier pointed up some stairs. "Second door on the right." Allie thanked her and jogged up the stairs, Marcus close behind.

"It could happen to anyone."

Why was he still defending Carly? "She was in there just chatting. The man we have been searching for isn't even there but she's having cake and coffee! If she wanted to have dessert with the woman, she could've at least called us to let us know."

Marcus stopped her at the top of the stairs. "Why don't you just cut her some slack? You were a rookie too and not that long ago as I recall."

"I wasn't *that* bad Marc. She acts like she

knows it all. I was teachable, she isn't. She's just annoying." Allie went down the hall. The office door was slightly open and someone was talking inside. She recognized the voice. She raised her hand for Marcus to be quiet. She nodded for the door and took out her gun.

Back pressed against the wall, she inched her way to the portal. She peeked around the corner and listened. Someone was calling the police. As soon as she heard the badge number she relaxed and put her gun away. "It's Nate."

"Nate?" Marcus frowned and put his gun away. "What's he doing here?"

"Let's find out." Allie pushed the door open. "Knock, knock."

Nate spun around and stared at her a few seconds before he relaxed. His phone still to his head. "I'm on hold. Can you believe it?"

"Actually, I can." Allie looked at Willard's limp body and shook her head. "We didn't get here soon enough." Allie watched Marcus walk over and check a pulse. With the amount of blood and the obvious gunshot wound to the head it was doubtful he survived, but they always hoped. Allie took a moment to look around the office. It was a mess. The trash smelled as if it'd been there for weeks. The dust was thick on every surface. "Why would anyone kill him?"

"Because he's a slob." Nate hung up the phone and sighed. "Help is on the way."

"What happened?" Marcus asked. "Did you find him or someone else?"

"No, I did."

"And?" Marcus was impatient. Allie

understood his reasoning, but Nate may take it the wrong way and they'd get nowhere.

"And he called it in, Marc. Why don't you go downstairs and keep everyone out of here? When CSU arrives we'll see if anyone heard or saw anything."

"Why can't he answer a simple question? Does he have something to hide?" Marcus asked waving his hand in Nate's direction. He came around the desk, standing tall next to her. What had gotten into him?

Nate straightened. "I don't like what you're implying. Are you trying to say *I* did this?"

"Most times when a suspect can't answer a simple line of questioning, yes that's what I begin to assume. Guilt prevents people from giving honest answers. They avoid questions, only give partial truths."

"I didn't do this!" Nate narrowed his eyes, his face inches from Marcus. "Watch yourself, *Detective* Marcus."

"Or what? You'll kill me too?"

"All right, that's enough!" Allie pushed herself between the two of them. She turned to look at Marcus, holding him back. "Go outside. Now. Cool off."

"Oh come on! I'm just asking a simple question! Why can't he answer it?"

"You're too close to this, Marc. Get out!" Marcus hesitated and she narrowed her eyes at him. "I mean it. Now."

Marcus's jaw clenched, his hands were fists at his side. "Fine." He spun on his heel and marched out of the room.

Allie sighed and ran a hand through her hair. "Sorry." She turned and faced the man. "He gets worked up at crime scenes sometimes." Resting her hands on her hips, she looked at the desk cluttered with paper. "What were you doing here, Nate? What happened to the assignment you said you had to get done?"

Nate shrugged. "It didn't take me as long as I thought." Nate cleared his throat and crossed his arms over his chest. "You think I had something to do with this."

It wasn't a question. A straight accusation. Allie was ready to answer. "Prove him wrong. Tell me what happened. Why are you here before us? You knew we were going to question him."

"It's the middle of the afternoon. Why would he be home? You never told me you were going to his house. You said you were going to question him. When I got to the precinct, I found the note on your desk of his name. I looked it up and found he worked here." Nate held out his arms. "Here I am. I came up here and now he's dead."

"Interesting choice of words." Marcus leaned against the door jamb.

"You know what? I don't have to put up with this. I'll give my statement at the precinct." Nate pushed past Marcus on his way out.

"Why was he here? This isn't his case."

"He's just here to help! Why do you act like that?"

"I don't like him. Something isn't right."

"Stop treating him like a criminal. He's a good guy. He explained to me what happened and it all makes perfect sense so knock it off." Allie glanced down the hall. "Is CSU here?"

"Yes. I called Ashton. He'll be here in a few minutes."

"Did you tell him your suspicions?"

"No."

"Good. You don't want the *entire* precinct thinking you've gone nuts." Allie leaned against the wall. "How could you even *think* it was Nate? He's done nothing but help us."

"You're blinded because you like him. If he were a woman, you'd think something was off too."

"You're just jealous."

"Of what? What does he have that I want? Nothing." Marcus stepped into the hall. "Here they come. We'll talk later."

"No. We won't talk later. Until you can act like an adult, I don't care to talk to you anymore."

Allie moved down the hall away from him. He could talk to CSU. Allie passed Dana on the stairs.

"Hi Dana. Marcus is waiting for you."

"Thanks Allie."

Allie reached the bottom of the stairs and looked for Nate. There was no sign of him. Frowning, she went outside. Gone. With a sigh, she went over to an officer to get a ride. She needed to find him. She had a lot to apologize for.

*****

"Is it done?"

Nate glanced behind him before switching lanes. "Yeah, it's done. Barely made it out. Marcus and Allie got there sooner than I expected."

"As long as it's done, I don't care. I have an assignment but I won't be able to give it to you yet." He hesitated. "Is that a problem?"

The thought of spending more time with Allie brought a smile to his face. "No, that won't be a problem at all. I'll just stick around the precinct."

"Don't get too comfortable. I mean it."

"Right."

"I don't want another Blake Finney accident."

"I know. I'm heading back to the precinct. I was the first on scene so I need to give a statement." Nate flipped on his blinker and exited the interstate. "It shouldn't take more than an hour or so and I'll come check in."

"I'll be waiting."

Nate hung up and tossed his phone in the seat next to him. This job was getting old. What used to be a carefree job was beginning to get stressful. The more assignments he had, the more he wondered if he would've been better off accepting

the original punishment. The assignments were

getting riskier. Working with Allie seemed all right

but no doubt Marcus would soon put all of the

pieces together. What would happen when that day

came?

*****

Bastian watched them through the

bookshelves. Allie was happy today. *She knows its*

time. Bastian couldn't stop the smile that came to

his face. She wore her blue peacoat today. When

she first bought it he hadn't liked it. The bright blue

didn't fit her personality. Yet, the more she wore it,

the more he liked it. It'd become his favorite. She

knew. She wore it for him.

She unbuttoned her coat slowly, as if teasing

him. Draping it on the back of the chair, she sat

down next to Nate. Allie handed him two files. Nate seemed less than enthused. He took out his phone and showed it to Allie. Allie's hand covered her mouth as she laughed. Bastian narrowed his eyes, his pulse picking up speed. This would not continue. It was time for her to see just how wrong Nate was for her. How right he was. Bastian looked down at the padded envelope in his hand. No more gifting from a distance.

It was a cold day. The snow had been falling for close to an hour. The ground was beginning to turn white. Just like the day they'd first met. Allie was so sweet. He'd come to deliver a package to her captain that day. Most people ignored him. Not Allie. She'd made him a cup of hot chocolate; told him to warm up before going back out. Their first date. His sweet, thoughtful Allie. His second chance.

*****

"Thanks for playing this down. I know Marcus really upset you earlier." Allie rested her hand on Nate's arm. "You're a good man."

"I don't know about that." Nate hesitated, his eyes locked with hers. "You make me want to try though."

She wasn't usually one for sappy one-liners, but the look in his eyes made her heart melt. Allie cleared her throat. "We need to talk about the case."

Nate nodded. "Right. What about it?"

"Willard Gates was our only lead on this, but there has to be something we're overlooking. There is no such thing as the perfect crime."

"Well, yet." Nate smiled and leaned forward slightly. "I haven't committed it yet."

Allie rolled her eyes and playfully pushed him back. "Knock it off. I'm serious." Allie couldn't stop the smile that came to her face. "Here are the case files. There are five total. You look at these two and I'll look at the other three." Allie handed him two folders before opening her first one and reading the same words she'd read at least ten times before. She'd have the reports memorized before long.

All of the evidence was the same. Allie read the rundown of the scene and paused. "Nate?"

"Hm?"

"The scene was wiped down." Allie pushed the first file aside and opened the second one. "This one was too. Why were the crime scenes wiped down?"

"To get rid of prints." Nate frowned,

shaking his head. "What does it matter?"

"It matters because it means our killer has something to hide. He's in the system. That means he must have killed before and been caught. If he's been caught once, he can be caught twice!" Allie pulled her phone out of her coat pocket. "I need to call Marcus."

An older woman walked by and cleared her throat. "No cell phones in the library."

"It'll just take a minute."

She pointed at a sign to prove her point. "Cell phones on silent. Unless you can communicate without talking, take it outside."

Allie rolled her eyes and stood up. "I'll be right back, Nate." Allie felt a bit rebellious and started dialing Marcus on the way out, glad he answered before she was able to get outside.

"Marcus."

"Marc, it's me. I think I found something. Have we checked this M.O. in the database?" Allie got two stern looks from the librarians at the check-out desk but chose to ignore them.

"Yeah, no hits."

"What about the gun?" Allie pushed the door open and went down the five steps to lean against a pillar.

"I haven't gotten that report back yet. Why?"

"I think our killer has been caught before. He wiped the scenes down." Allie listened to Marcus sigh. "Do you agree?"

"You're reaching, Allie."

A strong wind blew from the north. Goose bumps popped up on her arms. She'd hoped this conversation wouldn't take long. The mood Marcus had been in lately, she should have known he'd argue. "Marcus, will you just…"

"Calm down." She could hear the smile in his voice. "I didn't say I wasn't going to triple check everything. I'm just saying you're reaching."

"Thanks, Marc. You won't regret this!" Allie hung up and turned around. Nate stood on the top step, stiff as a board. "What are you doing? I was just on my way back inside."

"I'm sorry to do this." Nate held up her coat. "Put the coat on, we're going for a ride."

Allie frowned. "What are you talking about? We've just found a major piece to the puzzle."

"I'd do as the man says, Allie." Bastian stepped around Nate. He had a gun stuck in Nate's side.

Immediately her training kicked in.

"Sebastian, you don't want to do this. Whatever happened, we can fix it." Allie dialed her phone. She wasn't sure who she was calling, but as long as someone heard her, that's all that mattered. Keeping her eyes fixed on Bastian, she set her phone down on the step, keeping her hands up.

Bastian clenched his teeth. "My name is not Sebastian!" He emphasized every word by hitting Nate with the barrel of his gun.

"All right, all right. I'm sorry. I'm terrible with names. I can't remember my own sometimes." Allie glanced at Nate and saw the trust in his eyes. He gave a faint nod and looked over at her phone.

Bastian glanced around. From the satisfied look on his face, she knew no one was paying any attention to them. "Turn around."

"This isn't a good idea. We're both cops. Any second now this library will be swarming with cops. Do you really think you'll get away with this?"

Nate gasped as the barrel was stabbed into his ribs again. "I'm not afraid to pull the trigger. He means nothing to me. Turn around. Hands open where I can see them."

Allie sighed and turned her back to him. She kept her hands open at her sides. She looked around to find the street empty. Where was everyone? This wasn't some Podunk town in Kansas. This was the city. Where were all the people? She heard a jackhammer and winced. Construction. The street had been blocked off forcing people to go out of their way. Now what?

She heard them moving toward her. Allie's

mind scrambled. No doubt he'd take her gun. He would be caught off guard. Allie knew that was her moment to act. Closing her eyes she took a deep breath and waited. As soon as she felt the light touch at her side, she grabbed his hand and twisted it around behind her back.

In an instant, he retaliated and in seconds she was on her back, pinned to the ground. She gasped for air, staring at her abductor. Bastian stood next to Nate who was pinning her to the ground. "Nate? What are you doing?"

Nate held her gun to her head. "You should know better, Allie. Nice and easy now." Nate jerked her up off the pavement, twisting her arm behind her back. "Where to?"

"You're hurting her!" Bastian's hand gently rested on her shoulder. He looked at her, an unexpected tenderness in his eyes.

"You wanted me to immobilize her, that's what I did. Where to?"

"Around the corner." Bastian ordered and they moved that way. Allie looked around for someone. Anyone. Her mind scrambled. How could Nate do this? How could he hurt her? Why did Bastian want to hurt her?

They turned the corner and in the alley was a brown van. The only thing that appeared to be holding it together was rust. Nate opened the passenger door. The shrill shrieking of the door made her cringe. "Get in." He motioned inside. Allie hesitated. "Don't fight this, Allie. Just get in the truck."

If she turned and ran she wouldn't get far, but she might get far enough to alert someone. They would kidnap her whether she came quietly or not. Marcus always teased her she would never be called quiet or soft spoken. Time to prove it. Allie turned and started running, She heard them chasing after her. They were faster. Allie screamed as loud as she could. A gunshot echoed through the alley.

<u>9</u>

Marcus pushed the food around on his plate. Angelino's was supposed to be the best Italian in town but he just couldn't bring himself to eat it. Something was off. He was missing something. Allie had found some luck with the crime scene being wiped down, but that was a long shot and he didn't hold out much hope. This case was cold. They were wasting their time. Their only break in the case in two months had been Willard Gates. In a matter of hours, their lead turned into a dead end. Literally.

"We didn't have to go out tonight, you know."

He sighed. "I'm sorry, Dana." He put his fork down and sat back in his chair. "I can't get this out of my mind. None of this adds up."

"Well, let's talk about it."

Marcus chuckled and leaned forward, his elbows resting on the table. "This isn't exactly first date conversation."

"It kind of is. I'm a medical examiner. You're a cop. It's what we do."

"I'll give you that." Marcus licked his lips and glanced around. "All these people go about their lives not realizing all the horror that goes on around them. It's crazy. They read the crime reports for their neighborhoods thinking they're safe, but they're not."

"That's why you have a job." Dana took a bite of a breadstick. "Come on, talk to me."

"Have you met this new guy Allie's been hanging around with?"

"Mm." Dana nodded and swallowed her food. "Nate Harris. He's cute."

"Thanks for that." Marcus said rolling his eyes. "I don't like him. There's just something about him." Marcus hesitated and laughed humorlessly. "Did you know he was at that crime scene first this afternoon?"

"What does that matter? He's a cop."

"Allie said he had another assignment so he wasn't coming to meet with Willard. Yet, he just happens to be at the store where Willard works? And Willard ends up dead? It doesn't make sense. How did he know where Willard worked? Why did he decide to go there? Not to mention I haven't even heard of this guy; not until this investigation opened up."

"Did you ask him?"

Marcus nodded. "He got defensive and Allie got mad. She always takes his side."

"You're jealous."

Marcus sat back, throwing his hands in the air. "Why does everyone think that? Don't you think this is all a little suspicious?"

"It is, but you're taking it to extremes Marcus. Do you know Jake Kensington?"

He shook his head. "Never heard of him."

"He's a cop. He's been on the force for thirteen years. Just because you haven't heard of someone doesn't mean they're bad people."

"All right, I get that. But it still doesn't explain why he was at that crime scene today."

"Stop being so suspicious of him. Take the man out for a coffee. Visit with him a bit and maybe once you get to know him you'll see he's not so bad. I've heard good things about him."

"From Allie?" Marcus sighed and shook his head. "I *do* need to get a better attitude. But really, he isn't as wonderful as everyone is making him out to be!"

Dana laughed outright. "All right, this is obviously upsetting you. Buy my dinner and go back to the precinct. Maybe you'll find something useful."

"I'm sorry. This is the worst date ever. I'm in a sour mood. I should have rescheduled with you."

"On the contrary." Dana smiled. "This has been quite entertaining."

Marcus chuckled and pulled his vibrating phone out of his pocket. "Well I'm glad you can find such enjoyment at my obvious distress."

"Anytime." Dana laughed and finished her water.

Marcus chuckled and held his phone up for Dana to see. "Can you believe this?" Marcus clicked to answer the phone. "Nate. Were your ears burning?"

"Marcus, it's Allie." Her voice was just above a whisper.

"What?" He exclaimed and sat forward. "Why are you calling me from Nate's phone? Where are you?"

"I don't know." Tears in her voice. Allie never cried. She was terrified. "He threw me in the van and…"

Marcus heard yelling in the background followed by banging noises. "Allie?" Marcus paused, listening. The line was dead silent. "Allie!"

He looked at the phone. Call ended.

Dana leaned forward. "Marcus what's wrong?"

His breathing labored, he closed his eyes and prayed as he tried to call the number back. *Please. Let this be a bad dream.* The phone rang. Once. Twice. *Please pick up. Please pick up.* Three. Voicemail.

"Marcus, what is it?"

He hung up the phone. "He took her." He stared at his phone in disbelief. She was gone. He stood up and reached for his wallet. He threw a large bill down on the table. "There's for the check. I'll be calling you later. I might need your help." Marcus hurried to the door. He fished his keys out of his pocket and dialed Carly. He would find Allie and when he did, Nate would be sorry they'd ever met.

* * * * *

"You shot him!" Allie launched herself at Bastian. She got a few good hits in before he overpowered her. She'd never felt so helpless. Bastian pushed her down in a chair. His hold on her was strong but gentle. He used zip ties to restrain her.

"You could have just come with me. Why didn't you want to come?"

Allie stared up at him. He looked hurt. He had kidnapped her and he was upset because she'd hurt *his* feelings? "Why did you force me to come?"

Bastian sighed. "I didn't think I'd have to."

He was like a child, pouting at the table. Allie took a calming breath. Whatever fantasy he thought she would fulfill, she needed to play along.

If she did, she'd live longer. She could earn his trust and at least help Nate who was in the closet dying from a gunshot wound. "You scared me. *He* scared me." Allie pointed at the closet where Nate coughed and gasped. "What was I supposed to do?"

He nodded slowly. She could almost see the wheels turning in his head. "I guess you're right. I didn't mean to scare you." He came over and knelt down on the floor in front of her, taking her hand in both of his. "I just wanted to surprise you!" His smile stretched across his face. "You've been waiting so long; I thought you'd be excited I had come."

"That's just it. It's been so long, I thought you'd left me." Nothing she said was a lie but she knew he would take it differently than she meant it. Now that she knew Bastian was the stalker, a lot of things were coming together making her feel incompetent.

"I'd never leave you." Bastian stood up and went to the cabinet. "Thirsty?" He pulled two cups from the cabinet. Plastic cups. He went to the refrigerator and pulled out a can of orange soda. The tension eased from his shoulders. He smiled sheepishly. "I got your favorite." The can popped loudly as he cracked it open. He poured it in the cup and it fizzed up to the top in seconds.

"What do you want?"

"What do you mean?" He handed her the cup.

Allie looked at the sparkling contents and wondered if she should drink it. She was thirsty. It'd been hours since she'd had anything to drink. The tantalizing orange scent wafted up to her, beckoning her to take a sip. *He wouldn't risk taking me and Nate and holding us here just to kill me.* Allie took a sip with reluctance. The cool liquid felt good on her dry mouth. She took another sip, a bigger one this time. The soda popped and fizzed in her mouth.

"What are we going to do?"

Bastian seemed delighted at the question. "There's something I want to show you." He took the cup from her and put it on the counter.

A moan sounded from the closet and Bastian kicked the door. Allie winced and looked down at her hands. "Will you let me help him?"

His eyes went dark. "Why do you want to help *him*?"

Allie swallowed hard, choosing her words carefully. "He works with me. He's my partner in a case. It's part of my job to look out for my partners." Allie met his eyes. "He's my friend."

Bastian hesitated then groaned. "Fine. Make it quick."

"My hands." Allie held out her restrained wrists.

"Make do." Bastian yanked the door open and Nate's limp body fell out.

Allie went over to him and knelt down. "It's going to be all right. Hang in there." Allie looked up at Bastian. "I need towels and water. Please."

Bastian hesitated, narrowing his eyes at her. "Fine."

As soon as he left the room, Allie looked at Nate. "I need answers." Allie pulled his shirt open, some of the buttons snapped off and scattered on the floor. She pulled the shirt back from his wounded shoulder and winced at the angry redness. "Why were you helping him?"

"It was an assignment. I didn't want to."

Allie hit him. "Then why *did* you? I thought I could trust you. We could have taken care of him together."

"I told you it was fine. I nodded." Nate gasped as she put pressure on his wound. "I told you to make the move, but you didn't."

"I couldn't risk you getting shot. Now I see that didn't matter."

"The gun he had wasn't real. It was a pellet gun. If you trusted me, you would have made the move."

Allie glanced down the hall Bastian had disappeared in. He wasn't coming. Allie pushed down on the wound, harder than necessary. Nate gasped. "Don't act like that. If the situation had been reversed you would have done the same thing. And what do you mean it was an assignment?"

"Do you have to do that?" He whined.

"I have to stop the bleeding." Allie ripped off the bottom of Nate's shirt and pressed it into the wound.

"This was my good shirt!"

"It already had a bullet hole in it. Get over it." Allie heard footsteps. "He's coming back. Is there any way out of here?"

"I don't know. I'd been shot, I wasn't exactly looking." Nate took several slow breaths, his hands clenched at his sides. The pain in his eyes tugged at her heart. She had to do something to help him. Her resources were limited here.

Bastian came back into the room carrying a

white towel, some water, and a knife. Allie was aware of every move he made with the knife.

"Clean it with this." Bastian dipped the towel in the water and wrung it out. "He'll bleed to death if we don't stop it."

Allie took the towel from him. She tossed the torn shirt piece aside and pressed the towel to the wound. Nate screamed in pain. His body trembled. "I'm sorry. Hang in there." Bastian stood up and went to the stove. He turned on a burner and put the knife in the fire. "What are you doing?"

"I'm going to stop the bleeding."

"Why are you helping him?"

Bastian looked down at Nate, then back at her. "*I'm* no killer. If he's your friend, I'll help you save him."

Should she trust him? Bastian left the knife

sitting in the fire and disappeared down the hall again. "Who is he, Nate? Really?"

"I don't know."

"You helped him! How could you help him kidnap me if you don't even know him?"

"It was…"

"An assignment." Allie sighed. Nate wasn't helping at all.

"I had two choices. This one seemed the better choice."

"What was the other choice?" Allie couldn't wait to hear this. Kidnapping was a better choice?

"Kill him. I couldn't just kill him."

Allie shook her head. "No, instead he'll just kill me."

"I won't let that happen."

"Right, as he's lying on the floor dying he

promises he won't let me die." Allie scoffed.
"Thanks that's reassuring."

Bastian came back with medicine and a bottle of alcohol. He took a bottle of water from the refrigerator and came to kneel next to Nate. "Move back." He took four pills from the bottle and set it aside. "This is a pain reliever. Take it." Nate hesitated only a second before opening his mouth. Bastian put the pills in and gave him a drink. "I'll wait a moment to let that take effect."

"Take effect? What are you going to do?" Allie was thankful he was helping, but scared to know the kind of help he was offering.

Bastian pulled tweezers out of his pocket. He poured alcohol on the wound and tweezers. "I'm going to cauterize it."

Her eyes grew large and she grabbed his arm

to stop him. "You can't do that. You could really hurt him."

"I do that or he dies."

"Can't you just let him go?"

Bastian pressed his lips together and shook his head. "No one would find him out here. He wouldn't make it half a mile down the road. This is the best option."

"But this is the 21st century! Surely there is something we can do other than this!"

"Give me a better option and I'll do it. I need to get the bullet out." Nate's screams filled the house as Bastian used the tweezers to remove the bullet.

Her stomach churned. What had they gotten themselves into? She'd never felt so scared and helpless in all her life. What would Marcus do right now? He'd pray. She hadn't prayed in years. God wouldn't want to hear her now. *Marcus, I need you. You have to find me. Please.*

*****

"What I need are answers and you're not giving me any." Marcus moved the phone to his other ear and got out of the car. "Did she make any other calls? Where was she at? I want to know what she was doing from the time she woke up until the time she was taken."

"Well there isn't a lot to tell. I told you I don't think Nate could have done this." Carly was adamant. "Someone else has taken Allie. I went back through what I know about her day. We put a trace out on her phone and they went to pick it up. According to phone records, she called you and she called me."

"And you didn't pick up?"

"Well, I did, but I heard talking and she wasn't talking to me, so I just hung up. I figured it was an accident."

Marcus closed his eyes and pinched the bridge of his nose. "Right. Because she does that all the time." He was beginning to understand why Allie got so frustrated with Carly. "Listen, I'm at Allie's now. They've been searching the scene so I'll see what they've found. Where did they locate her cell phone?"

"Elm Street. Uniforms found it with a couple of teenagers. They were trying to sell it for a hundred bucks."

"Bring them in."

"Already took care of that. They'll be here any minute and ready for interrogation."

Marcus thanked her and hung up before stepping into the house. He looked around. Nothing seemed different or out of place. He went to the kitchen and found Simon. "Find anything?"

"Nothing. No signs of struggle. There was no way she was taken here."

Marcus sighed, running his hand through his hair. "Something's gotta give here." He took a moment to look around the room. Allie was meticulous. She tidied her house every day; had a fit when he put his feet on the coffee table. Marcus looked at the floor. There was dirt on the floor but not enough to make him question. CSU could have tracked most of the dirt inside.

He moved to the front room. Something was out of place. Marcus scanned the room, taking in every detail. The picture. He went to the end table and picked up the picture frame. A picture of herself. She was staring directly into the camera. Allie hated getting her picture taken. Why would she allow it? Why didn't she block the camera? Unless she didn't know it was a camera. Marcus got a sinking feeling.

Images flashed through his mind of times Allie had been on edge, looking over her shoulder. Was someone stalking her? Marcus shook his head and put the picture down. Crazy. Allie would have told him. This picture could easily be from her college friends. Marcus moved to the bedroom to see how much progress the team had made.

10

Allie sat on the bed with her legs crossed, her eyes memorizing every detail of the room. It wasn't hard. It was an exact replica of her bedroom. It'd taken a few minutes for the shock to wear off, but now, she had to focus. There was a window. The window was plastic. The picture in the window was exactly what she would see out her bedroom window at home.

He'd been in her bedroom.

A shudder went down her spine. If someone asked her last week who knew her the best, she would have said Marcus. Now she wasn't so sure. Allie closed her eyes and took a deep breath. "Focus, Allie. Focus." She whispered and opened her eyes.

Bookcase next to the window. Books were weapons. The books were real but she couldn't pull them off the shelf. The case itself was bolted to the wall. No help.

Nightstand. Not bolted to the floor, but too bulky and heavy to do anything with. Allie frowned at it. She might be able to take it apart. Biting her lip she considered how hard it would be to take apart with no tools. Maybe not worth the effort.

Alarm clock, potential weapon.

Bed. Sheets could be used as a distraction, a restraint, or a weapon. It was an old spring bed with no box springs. When Bastian went to bed, that would give her ample time to work one of the springs loose. Bed could be a possible weapon. Allie stood up. Now was the time to act.

*****

Bastian paced his bedroom. The plan was falling to pieces. He'd never meant to shoot anyone. It'd been an accident. Pursing his lips he stopped in front of the window. He raised his arm and leaned against the window sill staring at the field that stretched for miles behind his house. Allie had been upset. Would she forgive him for hurting her friend?

Resentment boiled up inside him. He never should have allowed Nate to come. He'd wanted to prove to Allie Nate wasn't the right man for her. Instead, he'd managed to prove that *he* wasn't the man for her. Bastian pushed away from the window and started pacing again.

He'd helped Nate. The man was no longer bleeding. Bastian paused. He'd made a mistake and fixed it. Surely Allie saw that and understood. Hope rose in his heart and he smiled. "She'll see it."

Bastian went to the closet and pulled out the lavender dress. Soon she'd be ready. A smile came to his face as he put the dress back and closed the door without a sound. She'd be beautiful again and this time, he'd be the one she danced with.

*****

Marcus left the room, slamming the door behind him. He dropped the file on his desk and fell back in his chair. He rubbed his face, his mind blank. Every lead was coming up empty. No one saw or heard anything. The teens who took the cell phone claimed they found it at the library. Questioning the librarians had been no help. Only one remembered Allie and that was only when Allie had attempted to make a phone call.

He leaned back in his chair; his hands

formed a steeple in front of his mouth. What was he missing? Allie would be able to see it. Marcus closed his eyes and rested his head against the back of the chair. He would make up a story and Allie would take something from that story to solve the case. He had to make up the story.

"Marcus!"

Marcus jumped at the loud voice behind him. The jolt sent him toppling backward out of his chair. He winced and glared up at his sister laughing above him. "What are you doing here?"

"You haven't been home for almost two days."

Marcus sighed and closed his eyes. He covered his face with his hands as his head started to pound. He wiped his hands down his face and groaned. "I'm sorry."

Maddie sat down on the floor beside him, her back leaning against his desk. "I heard about what happened with Allie. No luck yet?"

Marcus shook his head. "Nothing. I'm failing her. She's probably out there waiting for me right now and I've got nothing."

"Don't do that to yourself, Marc. You'll find her." Maddie hugged her knees to her chest, resting her chin there. "Can I help with anything?"

"I need food. I haven't eaten since yesterday."

"What do you want?"

"There's a Chinese restaurant a couple of blocks from here. Just tell him you're there to pick up for Marcus and he'll give you the food. If you want something go ahead and get it. My wallet's in my desk."

Maddie nodded. "Are you sure you'll be all right?"

Marcus swallowed hard. "Yeah." He croaked and glanced over at Allie's desk. Two days without her felt like an eternity. Marcus started to sit up when he spotted it. "What's that?" He crawled over to her desk and pulled the paper out.

"What is it?" Maddie came over to join him.

"I don't know." Marcus frowned at the wax seal holding the paper shut.

"That's old."

"The paper isn't. Who does this anymore?"

"Someone trying to be dramatic. Open it. Let's see what it is." Maddie bit her lip and leaned forward.

Marcus slipped his finger under the paper, releasing the wax seal. He unfolded the letter. The words made his blood run cold. He swallowed hard, his eyes slamming shut. She'd kept a secret. He clenched his teeth and stood up, looking for Carly. He whistled when he saw her and motioned her over. He slipped the letter into an envelope from his desk and handed it to her. "Get this to CSU and have it dusted for prints."

Carly started to open the envelope. He snatched it from her hand.

"No." He sealed it shut. "Do not look at it. Tell no one about it. I mean it."

"Fine. Gosh, I just wanted to look."

Marcus held the envelope out to her. "Well don't." Carly folded the envelope and shoved it in her back pocket before stomping to the elevator. It was becoming more and more clear to him why Allie found her so difficult to get along with.

Marcus turned to find Maddie sitting back in his chair.

"I'm sorry, I gotta go."

"What about your food?"

Marcus slipped into his coat and sighed. "Get me the food and I will come home tonight and eat it."

"Be there by six-thirty."

"I'll try my best."

*****

Allie heard talking outside. Bastian and Nate. What were they conspiring to do to her next? Nate groaned in pain and she sympathized. Why? He'd come to her as a friend and she'd trusted him. They'd worked side by side for weeks. He'd toyed with her emotions. Then he'd hurt her. Betrayed her. Why should she care at all about him? She had a plan. She couldn't waste her energy caring about the man who deceived her.

Allie picked up the side of the bed and moved it as far as she could before walking to the other side and doing the same. Walking the bed across the room was turning out to be more difficult than she first thought.

Footsteps. Slow. Even.

She didn't have much time. She had to keep moving it. Only four more turns and the bed would be close enough to the door to block it. Moving as fast as she could, she got the bed as close as possible.

Metal scraped against metal as the key went into the lock. Allie picked up the pillowcase she'd loaded with springs from the bed and the handles from the night stand. She readied herself for the fight.

The lock clicked.

She moved behind the door.

The knob turned and the door opened only an inch before it hit the bed. "What?" A thud sounded before the door started banging against the bed. "Allie, come let me in!" She could hear his anger through his clenched teeth.

"If you want me, come in and get me."

Bastian growled and slammed the door against the bed. The bed moved, allowing the door to be opened a few more inches. His leg came through the opening and he kicked the bed back until he could open the door enough to get through. As soon as he appeared, she swung the loaded pillowcase at his head.

He yelled and fell over the bed, landing on

the floor. He started to get up on his knees and she hit him again, as hard as she could. When he fell back, she ran across the bed and out the door. Allie pulled the door shut behind her and ran, tripping over Nate in the process. Allie glanced at him, and then struggled to her feet.

"Allie, help me."

Allie met his eyes and hesitated only a moment. "You're on your own." She hurried to the door and her eyes widened at the three locks. She'd never be able to find the keys in time. Her mind scrambled as she looked around. The kitchen. The door hadn't been locked.

Allie hurried back to the kitchen, glancing down the hall at the bedroom. The door opened and Bastian glared at her. Allie bit her lip, determined. She grinned at the single deadbolt on the door. A flip of the lock and she'd be free. Allie flipped the lock, twisted the knob and tugged on the door. It didn't budge.

"No." Allie heard Bastian coming up behind her. "No, no, no!" Allie looked at the door. Why wasn't it opening?

Bastian's hand wrapped around her wrist and she turned to hit him. He caught her hand with ease, slamming her against the door. "Did you really think it'd be that easy?" He growled and slammed her against the door again.

Allie swallowed hard, her breathing labored. "What do you want from me? Please just let me go."

"Let you go?" An arrogant smile came to his lips as he reached up to the top of the door and pulled down the sliding lock.

Allie's eyes slid shut. Foolish.

"Previous owners had this put in. Extra protection from burglars." Bastian pulled her away from the door. He spun her around, twisting her arm behind her back to hold her in place. He jerked the door open in one swift move.

The soft wind caused her hair to brush her cheek and forehead. The fresh air smelled wonderful. The sun warmed her skin. She looked out at the golden wheat waving at her from the fields as if mocking her. "Will you please just let me go?" She whispered.

"So close, and yet so far." His hushed voice, so close to her ear sent a chill down her spine. The door slammed. The locks clicked.

*****

Marcus frowned at the number flashing on

his phone. He hated getting calls from numbers he didn't recognize. What if it was a call about Allie? Sucking in a deep breath he took the call. "Marcus."

"Detective Marcus, how nice to hear your voice again?" The female voice came across smooth and controlled.

"Who is this?" he demanded.

"Aw, you don't remember me? I felt I made a lasting impression."

"I really don't have time for this. State your business or I'm hanging up."

The woman sighed. "Fine. I have some evidence I want to share with you. I think you might find it helpful."

"Evidence for what?"

"Katie Thompson's murder."

"Daddy Cain?"

"Meet me in one hour if you want it."

Marcus hung up and stared at the phone. He had too much on his plate right now. He wanted nothing more than to find Allie, but that wasn't his only case. Marcus slipped the phone into his pocket before turning his attention back to Allie's bed.

Underneath her bed had been a box of random items. With the new outlook on the case, he realized these items weren't random. They were gifts from a stalker. Not unlike their murder board, Allie had created a stalker board which he'd been able to put together. She'd been trying to find him on her own. Had she found him or had he found her?

11

Nate swallowed hard, his chest and head throbbed. The handcuffs securing his hands behind him rubbed his wrists raw. Never in his wildest dreams had he imagined it ending like this. He was trapped by a psychopath he'd been assigned to help take Allie. In his stupidity he'd done it. Of course, he hadn't been given much of a choice. The assignment was to get Allie out of the way. He could never kill her. She'd come to mean more to him then he'd intended. His boss would be furious to know.

He glanced over at her now, motionless, handcuffed to the bed and his heart ached. Bastian had knocked her out and taken her to another room in the attic after her attempted escape. That hadn't been a smart move, but it'd almost worked. She had so much fight in her. She didn't like to give up. He admired her for that. Most people would have mourned at their misfortune, but not her. She saw things differently.

If only she'd see him differently.

Her head moved and he heard her groan. Nate glanced at the door, listening for any noise that came from downstairs. The sun was just now starting to peak over the horizon. Bastian left about this time every morning. He closed his eyes, focusing on the noise below. He heard the door shut downstairs. Bastian had left. The house was quiet.

Nate shifted his body, working his legs underneath him. He rocked himself back and forth until he was able to get up on his knees. He wavered, struggling to catch his balance. Face-planting into the floor didn't sound fun. He scooted

across the floor on his knees, keeping as silent as he

could just in case Bastian was still in the house.

Allie's head lifted and he watched her arm

jerk. Nate got up next to the bed, his body fatigued.

He let his head drop down on the bed. Pain was

shooting up and down his spine. His hands felt as if

they would fall off at any moment. He swallowed

hard and tried to catch his breath. He turned his

head to face Allie. Her brown eyes stared

unwavering at him.

"I think he's gone." He whispered.

"What are you doing here?"

Nate frowned. "Chopping up nuts for a

Betty Crocker recipe."

It was Allie's turn to frown. "I could do

without the sarcasm." Allie looked at her wrists

handcuffed to the headboard. She tugged on them but they didn't budge. She groaned and looked back at him. "Seriously, why are you here?"

"You're not the only victim here. In case you forgot, he shot me and brought me out here too. You were lucky and got locked in a bedroom; I was locked in a closet, bleeding, left for dead."

"I helped you. He stopped the bleeding."

"Yes, and that felt like a deep tissue massage."

"Cut the sarcasm, Nate. I mean it. I can't tolerate it right now."

"Sorry. It's how I cope." His feet tingled as they started to fall asleep. He leaned back far enough to fall on his backside. He stretched his legs out in front of him, and then rested his head back on the bed. "Are you still mad at me?"

"Yes." She hesitated. "Maybe." She met his eyes and sighed. "Fine, I'm not *that* mad at you."

"But mad enough you were going to leave me behind."

Allie licked her lips. "I had a choice to make."

"So your choice was to leave me behind."

"You know what? Don't act so hurt about this. You had a choice too and your choice landed us both in this mess."

Nate wanted to tell her the truth, tell her everything, but he couldn't. If she made it out of this alive, she wouldn't last long with this knowledge. "You're right. I'm sorry." He watched her considering his apology. When she gave a short nod, he felt a little better. "What letter was he having you write earlier?"

He watched her gulp. "A letter to Marcus, telling him to leave us alone, that I'm happy here."

"Why would you agree to write that?" He exclaimed. "What if he believes it?"

"I'm trying to build a trust with this guy. I tried to escape so he doesn't trust me. Writing that letter the way I did is one way to tell him I want to stay." Allie met his eyes. "And Marcus knows me. He'll know something isn't right."

Nate smiled. "You put clues to our whereabouts in there."

"No, I put clues about Bastian in there. I just hope Marcus can understand them. I couldn't be too obvious about it and cracking codes isn't Marc's specialty."

"Is anything his specialty? He doesn't seem like the brightest detective."

"Don't say that!" Allie snapped. "Marc is a great detective; he just doesn't have very high self-esteem. He has to convince himself before he will say anything or agree with anything. That takes time, but rest assured, Marcus *will* find me. He's just devising a plan."

"Too bad he can't work a little faster." Nate sighed and looked around the room. "We need to get out of this. What's the plan, Al?"

"Well for starters, we need to get out of these cuffs."

"Did you ever mention anything to Marcus about this guy?"

"No."

"Regretting that now, aren't you?"

"Nate, stop it. If you can't open your mouth with helpful information, then keep it shut. I'm trying to fix a problem."

Nate closed his eyes as the throbbing in his head got worse. "Don't yell, please. You might make my head explode."

"How are you feeling?"

"Like a million bucks." He glanced up at her and smiled. "How are we going to get out of the cuffs? Do you have something to pick the lock?"

"No." Allie looked around the room. "Right about now I'm wishing I was one of those chic women who had to have the fancy hairstyles and clothes."

Nate frowned. "Fancy clothes and hair? Where did that come from?"

"They'd have a bobby pin or a piece of jewelry to pick the lock with." Allie said simply and continued surveying the room. "How much pain are you in right now?"

"On a scale of one to ten?" Nate shifted his weight and fell back against the bed. "I'd say eight." He groaned. "What do you need? I can get it."

"Check under the bed. Any springs?"

Nate looked at the box spring. "You're going to take the bed apart?"

"This bed has a box spring?"

"Yep."

Allie groaned. "I need something small. See anything?"

"What about a pin?"

"A pen? I don't think MacGyver could pick a lock with a pen."

"No, not a writing pen, I mean like a straight pin." Nate chuckled. "Although I think he really could."

"What?"

"MacGyver. He could definitely pick a lock with a pen."

Allie smiled. "You would be a fan."

"What about the pin?"

"Impossible."

"A nail?"

"I could use a nail." Allie looked around. "Where are you planning on getting that from?"

Nate nodded to the vintage curtain rod above the bedroom window. "Those curtains are at least 30 years old and probably weigh as much as you do. If it's nailed up there, I think I could get a nail when the bracket comes down. The wall is just sheet rock. It should come right out."

"Couldn't hurt to try. Let's do this before he

gets back."

*****

Waiting in line for the most anticipated roller coaster of the year and unable to cut the line, Bastian stared at the clock on the wall. Work had him chained to a desk today. After two missed packages his boss had given his route to someone else, leaving Bastian to catch up on paperwork. A lot of it was long overdue, but he hated this part of his job. All he wanted was to see her, hear her voice. He'd never missed someone so much before.

Bastian opened the drawer to his left and pulled out a picture. She'd been his best friend, his confidant. She'd loved spending time with him. She never would have run away. If it weren't for the accident, they'd still be together. His hand tightened on the frame. It split. The glass shattered when he slammed the frame in the trash. He sighed into his hands, his fingers shooting through his light brown curls.

His hands came to rest together in front of his mouth. He glanced at the trash can out of the corner of his eye. He could see the tip of the broken frame. What was he doing? Bastian swiped the frame from the trash and opened the back, removing the picture. There was a cut on the picture now from the broken glass. Her face had been unharmed.

"What is that? Is that your wife?" Bridget stood next to his desk, her hand on her hip. "She's pretty."

Bastian flipped the picture upside down on his desk. "It's nothing."

"Oh…okay. Well if you need to talk, let me know." Bridget smiled and went back to her desk to do her deskercises.

Bastian hated her deskercises. She looked like a chicken bobbing up and down. He turned his attention back to the picture. He slipped it securely in his desk drawer and looked back at his computer. He opened a new document and began to plan his evening with Allie. Only two hours until he got to see her. Though her attempted escape had cut him to the core, he still longed to see her. But first, he had to pass a message on to the man. He was getting too close for comfort.

12

Marcus stared at the clock. It had been three days since Allie's abduction. Just when he thought they were getting closer, they hit another roadblock. There was no proof she was even still alive. The FBI had come in and taken over a big part of the investigation, but he was still working it on his own.

He'd never worked a case alone before. He'd always had Allie. Since she left, he was no closer to finding the murderer they'd been tracking and he was no closer to bringing Allie back home. Was his entire career just a secondary act? How could he take credit for cases when obviously it was Allie that ultimately solved them for him? She was sharing her credit with him. Maybe he wasn't cut out for this kind of work.

Footsteps sounded in the bull pen, getting closer to him. He didn't want to talk to anyone and willed the steps to go past his desk. Nevertheless, they slowed when they got closer to him, stopping directly in front of his desk. Marcus looked up and saw the courier. He forced a smile and sat up straighter. "You're late today."

"Yes, but this is my last stop." Bastian's smile seemed as forced as his own.

Marcus nodded and signed for the package. Usually packages went to Allie. Had every package she received been a bad one? She'd kept all these things hidden from him for so long. She obviously had no faith in his detective skills either. Marcus handed the clipboard back to Bastian and took the package. "Thank you."

"Have a good evening, Detective."

Marcus leaned back in his chair, staring at the type font on the package. It seemed familiar. The font seemed to be from an old typewriter. His heart pounded against his chest. This was the same type font on the packages Allie had saved.

Alarmed, he sat up and jerked open his desk drawer, scrambling for some gloves. The cop in him knew to put gloves on before he ripped the package open. He found some gloves and pulled them on. Using a pair of scissors, he carefully cut the package open and peered inside.

All he found was a note. He delicately removed it from the envelope. What message was this guy trying to send? Maybe this message could help lead them straight to Allie. Marcus looked over the handwriting. He recognized it immediately. Allie wrote this. Frowning, he hunched over his desk to read the letter.

Marcus, I love him. I am not lost, I've been found. This is what we both want and we want to be left alone. I'm sorry to have left so abruptly. The work I did with you was just to pass the time until I was able to be delivered to my love. Don't be sad that I'm gone. Be happy that I am happy in my new house with the messenger of love. All the best, Allie K.

Marcus released a heavy sigh. This couldn't be true. She had to have been working an angle. But why would she agree to write this? Marcus rubbed his face in his hands. There had to be a reason. She must have left some clue in the letter. He read the note again. None of it sounded like Allie. A "messenger of love"? Why would she say that? She was "delivered to her love"? What was she trying to say? She was abducted by a cupid?

Shaking his head, he took the note and went to see the captain about it. Maybe Captain Ashton could help shed some light on the letter, see something he was missing. At any rate, the letter would be turned over to the FBI and it would be up to them to decipher what the letter meant, if it meant anything.

*****

"You got it? Be careful!" Allie couldn't believe this plan was actually happening right now. Nate had managed to stand up and get over to the curtains. As much blood as she saw on his shirt, she was surprised he could move at all. Desperate times. Biting her lip, she watched him take several deep breaths.

"I guess if it doesn't work, at least we tried,

right?"

"That's right. We have to at least try."

Nate closed his eyes then groaned. "I'm sorry, I have to tell you something first. Surely you know I didn't really want to do this. I'm trying to help you now and I feel that has to count for something."

"Yes, it's great. I appreciate it. Now come on. We need to get this done before he gets back. We don't have much time and you're injured and it will take longer." Now was not the time to have this discussion. She was still mad at him and she still felt he did have a choice. Why had he chosen to side with Bastian? What had she done that made him turn on her? She couldn't fathom it.

"On the count of three." Nate took a deep breath. "One." Another breath. "Two." He squeezed his eyes shut. "Three!" He pulled down, falling to his backside with force. He let out a wail as the curtain rod came crashing down with him. The heavy metal connected with his head, knocking his head into the window sill. His body went slack and fell the rest of the way to the floor.

"Nate?" Allie waited for a reply, her breathing became labored. "Nate, get up!"

The man didn't budge.

She heard a door close and looked at the window. That was a car door. Allie looked down at Nate. If Bastian came up here and saw him, what would she say? What would Bastian do if he realized they had been trying to escape again? There had to be something she could do. Allie tugged at the handcuffs again. "Nate! He's back, you have to wake up!"

She started to slip her shoe off her foot. She kicked it over at him. The shoe hit the ceiling and shot straight down to the floor. Groaning she slipped off her other shoe and stretched her leg out several times, aiming for Nate's head. This was her last chance. One even kick and the shoe flew through the air, colliding with Nate's torso. Still, the man didn't budge.

The front door opened downstairs and she knew her time was up. Bastian was back. He would come up and soon find out what they had done. What would he do to her? What would he do to Nate?

*****

Bastian went up the stairs to greet Allie. He had his list in hand of the things they could talk about tonight. It would be a night to remember! He smiled, smoothed his shirt and knocked on the door twice before unlocking it and going in. "Allie, I have a surprise for you."

His smile faded when he saw the curtain had fallen from the window and the sun was shining in Allie's face. He closed the door behind him and ambled toward the window. "I'm sorry. What happened to the—"

Teeth clenched, he frowned at Nate passed out in the mess of curtains. "What is he doing over here?" He demanded and looked at Allie for answers.

She opened her mouth and closed it several times before admitting. "He came over and tried to attack me. I kicked him and he hit the wall, pulling the curtain down with him. I guess it knocked him out."

Bastian's hands clenched at his side, crumbling the list into an accordion mess. "He tried to hurt you?"

"Yes, he did. He said since I was tied up, he may as well." Allie tugged at the handcuffs. "I couldn't get free."

Bastian noted her shoes on the floor by Nate. She was telling the truth. She had been attacked and it was partially his fault for leaving her defenseless and tied to the bed with no way to really protect herself.

A knock sounded on the door downstairs followed by the doorbell buzzing three times. Bastian's head whipped around and looked at Allie. "Who is that?"

Allie shook her head. "I don't know."

Groaning he marched to the door. He jerked

it open and turned back to Allie. "I'll take care of this and be back." He trudged down the stairs and went to the door. He peered around the curtain on the window and saw the young girl from the police station. She worked with Allie.

What was she doing here? He'd sent a clear message. Bastian clenched his fists. His body vibrated. Pure rage. He ripped the door open and Carly gasped, staring up at him in surprise. Two seconds later, she was pulling her gun out and pointing it at his head. Without a thought, he grabbed the gun from her hands, pulling her into the house and throwing her on the floor.

He slammed the door behind him. "Leave us alone! I told him not to bother us. I told *all* of you not to bother us!"

Carly got up on her hands and knees. "Why

did you do it, Bastian? You're such a nice guy!"

Bastian grabbed her up by the front of the shirt. "She's mine!" He threw her back on the floor. Her bag fell from her shoulder and papers dropped out of it. He saw a picture tucked under some of the pages and picked it up. It was the picture he'd sent to Allie. The last gift he'd given her. A picture of himself. Why did Carly have it?

Carly struggled to get up off the floor. He could hear Allie calling from the bedroom. Allie would have to wait. Bastian pushed Carly over onto her back and straddled her, holding the picture above her face. "What is this? Why do you have it?"

"Allie!" Carly hollered, looking behind her. Her eyes met his. "Where's Allie?"

Bastian grabbed her throat and squeezed.

"Why do you have this?"

"It's evidence. Marcus found it." Carly gasped.

Anger radiated through his veins. Allie had given it to *him*! Bastian crumbled up the picture and threw it in Carly's face. Standing, he paced. How could she do it? He had the picture back now. He could give it back to her.

No, she didn't want it. Bastian crossed his arms over his chest, his mind scrambling. What was he to do?

Shuffling behind him drew his attention and he saw Carly gathering up her papers. She hurried to the door, but he beat her there. "Not so fast. You've only just gotten here." The locks on the door clicked. One. Two. Three.

*****

219

Marcus all but ran to the elevator. He pushed the down button several times and waited two seconds before his patience wore thin. Groaning he jerked open the stair door and bolted down the steps. He burst into the room and went straight back to Dana's office. "Please tell me I misunderstood."

"I'm afraid not. Back here." Dana took him back to the autopsy room. He saw the body through the glass but it didn't register in his mind. "I'm really sorry, Marc. You don't have to come in if you don't want to."

"No, I'm coming in. I want to see what he did to her." Marcus stepped past Dana and went into the room. Her body was cold and lifeless on the table. "Cause of death?"

"Asphyxiation. I found this in her throat."

Dana held up a tray holding nothing but a ball of paper.

"What is it? Open it." Marcus looked down at the body again and touched her hair. She was so young. She'd been partly his responsibility and he'd let her down. How had he gotten to her?

"Marcus, it's two pieces of paper. One looks like a picture."

Marcus stepped away from the corpse and stood next to Dana as she used tweezers to carefully open the wads of paper. The paper ripped, making him jump. "This is going to take too long. There could be a clue on that paper."

"Just be patient. If you rush me, I'll ruin it."

"I'll go up and check on Harris. Text me when you're done." Marcus went over to the body on the table. He'd never expected to see her here.

What had she stumbled upon? What had gotten her killed? Marcus picked up her hand and lightly squeezed it. "I'm so sorry Carly. I *will* find him." He brushed some of the hair back from her forehead. He couldn't help Carly anymore, but he could help Allie. If Harris was out of surgery, he might be able to shed some light on who had Allie.

*****

Bastian removed the lasagna from the oven and set it on the table. Allie stared at it in surprise. "Did you make this?"

"No, your mother did."

Her blood ran cold. "She made it for you?"

"I get gifts from a lot of the people I deliver packages to. I've been saving this for a special occasion." Bastian sat down and smiled as he opened a bottle of wine.

Her mind scrambled to remember the gifts he'd sent her. He'd always sent them on special occasions. "Is this supposed to make up for my birthday?" She forced a smile, hoping it looked sincere enough.

Bastian's features softened. "Yes. I'm sorry things have been so rough lately, but we are together now, alone." He reached across the table and squeezed her hand. "Things will be much better now."

Allie nodded and took the glass he handed her. "To us, then?"

"To us."

The clink of their glasses echoed in the quiet house. Bastian had turned the lights down low so they could enjoy a romantic candlelight dinner. If he hadn't abducted her, this would have been a very romantic gesture. Table for two, dinner by candlelight, wine. Like déjà vu things came rushing back to her. This had been something she'd mentioned to a friend once. Her idea of a perfect date. Just how long had he been studying her?

"I thought, if you liked, we could watch a movie when dinner is over. I got a few movies from the rental store for you to choose from." Bastian seemed very proud of himself.

"That sounds perfect. Thank you." Allie leaned forward to take a bite, being stopped short by the chains around her waist. She stopped and tried to get closer but couldn't.

Bastian noticed her struggle and quickly moved to scoot her chair closer. "Sorry, I should have paid more attention."

"It's fine. Thank you." Allie took a bite of

her mother's lasagna. She didn't enjoy it as much as she used to. Would she ever be able to eat it again? Her stomach started to churn. He knew where her mother lived. Would he ever hurt her mother? What would she do? Allie tried to push the thoughts from her mind. She couldn't spend her days wondering if something would happen. She had to focus on what was actually happening.

One question still lingered in her mind: Where was Marcus?

13

"Detective?"

Marcus sat up and stifled a yawn. "Yes, I'm here." He rubbed his face and walked over to the doctor standing at the edge of the waiting room. "Is he out of surgery?"

"He is, but he's in pretty bad shape. We need to keep him medicated until his body has a chance to make a comeback on its own."

"What do you mean? Are you saying you put him in a coma or something?"

"Yes."

Marcus ran his hand through his hair. "You gotta get him out of it. There's a woman out there whose life depends on his testimony. I've got to find her and he was *with* her. He's the *only* person who can help me."

The doctor shook his head. "I'm sorry, it's already done. If we try to take him out, he may not be able to help you anyway. He lost a lot of blood; he has a concussion, a broken jaw, not to mention the beating he took. It looks like he got ran over by a truck. I'm sorry, but I can't help you." The doctor shrugged and disappeared down the hall.

"What now, Allie? Where are you?" Marcus made his way back to the morgue to see what Dana had found. Surely she had good news for him. He'd given her ample time to identify the picture she'd found.

*****

"As best I can tell, it looks like the picture is just a mistake."

"A mistake?" Marcus crossed his arms and

frowned at the computer as Dana brought up the image.

"Yeah, kind of like when you have your phone in your pocket and you accidentally take a picture. Only this picture was taken with an actual camera and it's just a picture of an arm. From what I can tell, it's a man's arm." Dana shook her head. "The image is so distorted. The other picture I found is just as bad." She switched pictures. "You see the man, but I can't make out a face."

Marcus frowned. "I recognize this picture. I've seen it before. Where is Carly's bag? Did they recover it?"

"I don't have it here. The FBI probably has it."

"I showed Carly the case file. I showed her the copy of the letter I received."

"What letter? From Allie?"

Marcus nodded and fished his own copy from his back pocket. "She wrote me this letter, apparently, asking me to leave them alone. It makes no sense to me. It's like she's writing a riddle."

"It's not a riddle, she's leaving you clues." Dana stood up and went to her desk, coming back with a pen. "She says in here that she was delivered to her love." Dana circled the word 'delivered'. "Then she calls him her 'messenger of love'. That is a clue as to who this guy is."

"Messenger. Delivered." Marcus's eyes closed. "Of course. It's that courier. He delivers all of the packages to the precinct. It's on his route but it's possible that's where he met her and became fixated on her. I just don't remember the guy's name! Carly figured this out and she went to confront the guy. She knew where Allie was and went to get her!"

Dana bent over the letter, reading it some more. "It says here something about a house. She's with this guy at his house. Do you know where he lives?"

"No, but I can sure find out." Marcus kissed Dana on the cheek. "Thank you!" He took the letter and ran out to his car. "Hang in there, Allie, I'm coming."

*****

Allie woke up and stared at the ceiling above her. She was alone. Nate hadn't been the best company, and certainly not the company she wanted, but he'd been someone to talk to. Was he still alive? Had Bastian killed him? It was all her fault. If she hadn't lied and said that Nate had tried to attack her, maybe he'd still be here. Maybe he'd still be alive.

Tears threatened, but she blinked them away. No, she did what she had to do to survive. She'd managed to gain Bastian's trust enough that she was no longer handcuffed to the bed. She was still confined to this third story bedroom, but she was able to move around.

Bastian had brought her some books to read. He'd left her some paper and every day when he had come home from work, she had a little letter for him to read. It pained her to write them, but it kept him happy and that was her focus until Marcus found her.

One week she'd been trapped here with him. It felt like months. She knew that a few more days trapped like this and her mind would make her believe this was the norm. Her mind would try to cope with the situation. It was Stockholm Syndrome. She would fight it as long as possible, but was it a hopeless battle? Would she be better off just giving Bastian what he wanted?

It was early in the morning and she could hear Bastian downstairs getting breakfast ready. Every morning he would bring her breakfast in bed. He would cater to her every need. Isn't that what most women dreamed of in a husband?

Footsteps approached. She heard Bastian set the tray down. He knocked twice before unlocking the door and coming in with the tray. A smile graced his face and he waited for her to sit up before he placed the tray in her lap and pressed a kiss to her forehead.

"Good morning, my love. Did you sleep

well?"

Allie nodded. "Yes, did you?"

"I thought of you all night." Bastian sat down on the edge of the bed and motioned to the tray. "Go ahead and eat."

"Thank you." Allie picked up a piece of bacon and took a bite. "Do you work today?"

"No, it's Sunday. The office is closed."

Sunday. She was abducted on a Monday. "What do you have planned for the day?"

"I don't know. I thought it might be fun to play cards or maybe watch some movies. What do you think?"

"Is it cold out? A picnic might be nice."

Bastian grinned. "A picnic would be nice. I'll have to check the weather. I got some more clothes for you since the days are getting colder.

When you get done eating and take your shower,
I'll show them to you."

"You didn't have to buy me clothes." Allie
smiled. "Thank you, that's sweet."

Bastian looked down and shrugged, pink
coming to his cheeks. "I wanted to. I'm so happy
you're here and enjoying yourself."

Her stomach started to churn when he
reached over and rubbed her leg. She wanted to jerk
her leg away, to throw the food at him and order
him not to touch her again. But she couldn't. She'd
seen Bastian's wrath and the harm it could do. She
didn't want to be the recipient of that, even by
accident. It was best to keep him happy. He hadn't
forced her to do anything; he was waiting for her to
make the first move.

All the while, she still watched outside for

Marcus's SUV to come tearing down the road to break her from this prison. It would be so nice to see him again, to look into his emerald eyes, to see that boyish, teasing smile that used to drive her crazy. She'd give anything to put up with his harassment right now. Any day now he'd be coming for her, a joke on the tip of his tongue. She just had to keep up hope.

*****

"I don't care if it's Sunday! I don't care if they're closed. You call the owner at home and tell him to get here, now!" Marcus hung up the phone and threw it on the dash. He leaned his head forward until it hit the steering wheel. Did no one else understand how important this was?

He'd heard the rumors around the precinct. Everyone thought Allie was dead already, but he knew better. Allie was a fighter. She was still out there. She would do whatever it would take to survive.

He sat back in his seat, staring at the messenger office. He'd gone around the precinct asking if anyone knew the courier's name. No one did. It made him the perfect perpetrator. He was the invisible man. He'd been in that precinct every day for the past several years and no one knew his name. Allie probably knew it. She knew everyone, remembered names...well almost.

"Sebastian!" Marcus grabbed for his phone. He dialed Captain Ashton. "Sebastian! She always called him Sebastian but his real name is Bastian! I just remembered! I was making fun of her because she got it wrong."

"Slow down, Marcus. What are you talking

about?"

"The courier. The guy who took Allie, his name is Bastian."

"Bastian? Let me write it down. They are still trying to get a hold of the manager or owner. I just got to the hospital. I'll call this in and hopefully we can get somewhere. Just sit tight."

"Is Nate awake?"

"No, not yet. They said they are waking him up today though. I'll call you if I learn anything."

"Thanks Cap." Marcus hung up and shook his head. How could he have been so blind? Had Allie figured out who he was? Had Allie gone to confront him but he had the upper hand? She never should have taken Nate with her if that was the case. He could have helped her better than Nate.

His phone started ringing and he glanced at

the Caller ID. He swiped his finger across the screen. "Ashton, does he know anything?"

"He's gone." Ashton sounded breathless. "They went in to wake him up, but he was gone. He left his bed made, the gown folded on top."

"Weren't there officers standing guard? How did he get past them?"

"We don't know. We're still learning that. I don't know why he would leave. It makes no sense."

He hated to ask. "Do you need me on this?"

"No. You stay where you are. I will call if anything changes."

Marcus hung up and rubbed his face in his hands. Why would Nate leave the hospital? It hadn't even been twenty-four hours since he'd been out of surgery. Where could he have gone? Marcus shook his head and continued to stare at the building, waiting for his phone to ring.

*****

Nate waited patiently. It would only be a matter of hours before he could leave. Until then, he had to get comfortable. Even with the pain medication, his body was still stiff and uncomfortable. Being up in the window sill wasn't the best idea and he feared his legs would give out on him before he wanted them to, but he was determined to try. He'd been given a new mission and he had to fulfill it.

He heard someone come into the room. He held his breath and closed his eyes focusing on stealth. Footsteps were coming closer. He opened his eyes, hoping it wasn't cleaning staff or something. No doubt the person would be committed to their job and clean the windows this time. He heard a swiping noise as they swept the floor. He counted his blessings.

The television clicked on to a football game. It was a man no doubt. This just might be his ticket out of here. Nate waited patiently. The man was humming as he emptied the trash receptacles. When he heard the man turn on the bathroom light, Nate carefully moved himself from the window sill to the floor. His body complained, but he kept going. He had to get out.

Nate glanced at the closed door, glad to see he had some privacy. He took a towel from the cleaning cart and twisted it in his hands. He stepped into the bathroom and saw the man bent over picking up some paper towel pieces from the floor. Nate tip toed over behind him and as soon as he straightened, Nate gritted his teeth and wrapped the towel around his neck.

Pain radiated through his entire body, but he willed himself to hold on. He had to. He'd been through worse. If he didn't complete his assignment, it would be his dead body they found next. His boss didn't appreciate jobs going undone. He was already behind schedule. The man stopped struggling and Nate let him go. The older man collapsed on the floor, his hat falling to the side.

Nate leaned against the wall, chest heaving. The pain meds couldn't overpower the exertion he was putting himself through. He would have time to heal later. Now was not that time. Nate took the janitor's coveralls off and slipped into them. He checked the man's shoe size. One size too big, but it was better than nothing.

After slipping into the shoes, he donned the man's old smelly baseball cap and went out into the room. He took the cart and pushed it out into the hall, heading for the exit, invisible to everyone he went by. Time to get to work.

14

Marcus leaned on the desk, trying to be patient as the manager looked over Bastian's employee file. They had one address for him. "I'll take it along with his full name and social."

The manager wrote down the information and handed the paper to Marcus. "I'm sorry it took me so long to get here. I had a long night, if you know what I mean." The man nodded and winked.

"Yeah, sure. Thanks for this. If you see him, call me." Marcus left his card and hurried out. Address in hand, he called in back up, flipped on his siren and went to find his partner. He'd finally caught his big break.

*****

It was late. Their third movie was almost

over. Bastian had gotten tired during the second movie and lay down on the couch, resting his head in her lap. He held her hand flat against his chest. Allie could feel the rhythmic beat of his heart. In sleep, his chest rose and fell peacefully. Allie looked down at his curly head in her lap. She moved her hand to his hair.

She pinched a piece of his hair between her thumb and forefinger, feeling its softness. She let it go and it fell back into place. Allie watched his eyes. He had beautiful blue eyes. She never used to like his hair, but it suited him. She gently brushed some of the curls from his forehead. They twisted around her finger bringing a small smile to her face.

Bastian's chest stopped moving.

Her eyes snapped to his to find him staring at her. Allie snatched her hand from his hair and averted her eyes. How could she be so foolish? Allie tried to focus on the end of the movie and ignore Bastian's eyes burning holes in her head.

Bastian sat up, and turned sideways on the couch facing her. His hand cupped the side of her face, his thumb grazing her cheekbone.

Allie met his eyes. Her heart kicked up a beat.

"Whitney." He breathed just before his lips captured hers.

Allie pressed her hands to his chest and pushed him back, frowning. "Whitney? Who's Whitney?" She demanded.

A look of horror crossed over the man's face. "I'm sorry. It was just a mistake. She's no one."

"No one?" Allie scoffed and stood up pacing

in front of the couch. "Who is she?"

Bastian's head dropped. "Someone I knew a long time ago." Bastian grasped for her hand. "Please, she means nothing to me. I have you."

Allie shook her head. "Our first kiss and you're thinking of someone else." She wasn't sure where the tears came from and she couldn't hold them back. "I thought you loved me."

"No, I do! I do love you, Allie!"

She swiped the tears from her face. "I just don't even want to look at you right now. I'm going to my room." Allie left the room and started up the steps.

Bastian made no move to follow her.

*****

"We've been here ten minutes and we haven't seen anything. Are you sure they're here?"

Marcus nodded. "This is the address his paychecks go to. We have to check it out."

Captain Ashton had convinced him that letting the FBI take point would be more beneficial and would bring Allie home sooner. He had yet to see those results. Allie had been missing a week and these rookies hadn't gotten any closer to finding her.

"All right, we'll go in, but you follow our lead Marcus, is that clear?"

Marcus nodded his agreement and followed the agents up to the house with his gun drawn. He checked all of the windows. If Allie were trapped in a room with a window she would have left some kind of sign to let them know. Nothing stood out to him. Still, this was Bastian's home. Where else could he be holding her?

The agents and Marcus each stood on one side of the door. The agents pounded on the door and announced themselves. Everyone stood in silence but there was no answer. With a single nod, an officer with a battering ram came up and knocked the door in. Agents swarmed the house, guns drawn, ready to fire. The house was cleared in a matter of seconds.

Allie and Bastian were nowhere to be found.

*****

Bastian hadn't brought her breakfast this morning. She'd stayed in bed, listening as he woke up and left. He woke up later than usual. Allie went and tried to open the bedroom door like she did every day, only this time it opened. She hesitated a moment, wondering if it could be true. She pulled the door open wide and saw the breakfast tray sitting in the doorway. A letter was on top of her cup of coffee with her name hand written on the front of it.

Allie bent down and retrieved the letter. She opened it and started reading Bastian's apology to her.

My dearest Allie,

I apologize for the mishap last night. Do not doubt for a minute that I love you. I wanted to tell you last night who Whitney was, but I wasn't quite ready to tell you. I say things better in letters, so please don't stop reading.

Whitney was my nanny when I was young. My parents never wanted a child, they were stuck with me and reminded me daily of all the things they could be doing if it weren't for me. They hired Whitney to raise me. They were never around. They provided enough money for Whitney and me to live happily.

When I was just fourteen, I told Whitney I loved her. She rejected me. I tried to talk to her, but she just wouldn't listen! She died in a car crash shortly after. My parents never came home and I was on my own. The checks still arrived and I was able to care for myself, but I never forgot Whitney. I never forgot how nice she was to me; how she took such good care of me, much like you did that day you gave me the hot chocolate when you knew I was cold.

While no one could ever come close to replacing my Whitney, I found myself in love with you from almost the first time we met. I don't want to be without you. I beg your forgiveness. I know in time, you will begin to see me for the man I am, the man you want to love. If you could find it in your

heart to forgive me, I will strive to earn that

forgiveness for the rest of my life.

Forever yours,

Bastian

Allie folded the note and wiped the tears from her eyes. The detective in her wondered if he had killed Whitney, but the woman in her only felt sorrow for this rejected boy. She wanted to help him, but how?

*****

Bastian got to work and trudged to his desk. He sat down and opened up his desk drawer, retrieving the picture of Whitney he'd stashed there days before. He ran his finger along the side of her face. "Sorry Whitney, time to go." Bastian tore the picture in four pieces and threw it in the trash. He had to give Allie his full attention now. She deserved that.

A commotion in the main office drew his attention. Bastian frowned and turned to see what was going on. His view was blocked by other peeping co-workers. Bridget was heading his way and he stopped her. "What's going on in there?"

"I don't know. Some detective is here talking to Simon." Bridget shook her head and walked to her desk mumbling. "Maybe he's here to talk to him about sexual harassment."

Sexual harassment? Not likely. Bastian turned back to his desk, his mind racing. Was it possible he was looking for Allie here? The man couldn't have her. He wouldn't let him. Bastian pulled up his computer and quickly deleted all of his personal files, his routes, everything pertaining to his life or work. He pulled a few files from his desk and tucked them into his messenger bag before slinging the bag over his shoulder and heading for the back door.

The office door opened and he glanced over his shoulder. His eyes were met by the man. They found him. Pushing Bridget down behind him to slow the man down, he hit the back door running. He hurried to his truck and kicked the beast into gear. Gun shots sounded but he continued to drive.

He glanced over his shoulder to see the man's outline disappearing. Pain seared through his arm and he glanced down to see a red stain on his shoulder. Wincing, he grabbed some napkins from the seat next to him and pressed them to his shoulder. Allie would know what to do when he got home. He had to get to her and leave before the man found them.

*****

Marcus raced after Bastian. He had a big head start but Marcus still had hope he'd catch up. He called in back up. They would be at the messenger company in no time going over Bastian's computer and files. His only job was to find where Bastian went.

His phone buzzed. "Go."

"We know where he's heading."

"You're a God-send. Shoot." Marcus listened as the Scott's fingers flew across a keyboard.

"His parents owned a house out west of town. It's an old farmhouse. That could be where he's been keeping her. It's a three story house. I'll send you directions."

"Thanks, I owe you one." Marcus hung up and waited for his phone to receive the incoming file. It couldn't get there fast enough. He had to get there before Bastian packed Allie up and made a run for it.

*****

Allie stood at the kitchen sink drinking her coffee and staring out the window. She was tempted to leave, but where would she go? It was cold outside. She didn't know where she was, and Bastian had treated her with nothing but respect. Why should she be so anxious to leave?

Her mind went to Nate. Was he still out there somewhere? He was such an odd guy. When he had first come in, she had seen him as a pimp. He turned out to be a friend through the investigation until Bastian had come along. How had Bastian been able to convince Nate to help him? Did Bastian know something she didn't?

Everywhere they had gone, people had greeted her but had nodded politely to Nate. No one knew him. He was from a different precinct, but it was hard to believe that he was unknown *everywhere* he went. Unless he wasn't a cop at all.

The roar of an engine cut into her thinking. She turned and went to look out the front window. Bastian's truck came roaring into the yard. Allie took her coffee cup back to the kitchen and left it in the sink. Bastian came in, blood-soaked napkins pressed to his arm.

"What happened?" She went over to him and pulled the napkins back to find a bullet wound. "You've been shot! Who shot you?"

"The man shot me. We need to go. They

found us."

"But your arm, you need a doctor."

"No time." Bastian marched down the hall to the bathroom. He slipped out of his shirt and tossed it aside. He started throwing some water on his arm to wash some of the blood off.

"Let me." Allie used a wash cloth to wipe away some of the blood. Bastian handed her some gauze and she pressed it into the wound. "Hold that." Taking his shirt, she ripped pieces of it off and wrapped it tight around his arm. "That will at least keep you from bleeding out. Where are we going?"

"I don't know. I have some money. We can just run away."

Allie's hands dropped to her side and she shook her head. "I have some questions first."

"We don't have time."

"Make time." Allie needed answers about Nate and she had a feeling Bastian knew more than he'd let on. "How did you get Nate to help you at the library?"

"I told him I'd tell you who he really was." Bastian tried to go past her but she stepped in his way.

"Who is he really?"

Bastian stared at her. "You really don't know?" He shook his head. "He's a killer, Allie. It's what he does."

"No." Allie frowned, her head rocked from side to side. "I don't believe you."

"Why do you think I acted so suddenly?" He scoffed. "He was going to *kill* you! I couldn't let him do that!"

"Oh, but you could lock me in a room alone with him? If he was a killer, why would you do that?" Allie stepped back, wrapping her arms around her middle, her mind racing through her time with Nate.

"You can think about this later, we have to go *now*!" Bastian grabbed her wrist and started down the hall, dragging her behind. He stopped short when his name was hollered below.

Allie's heart raced. She knew that voice. Marcus had come for her.

15

Marcus pulled up at the house and pulled out his gun as he hurried to the front porch. "Bastian Clark, this is the police! Come out or I'm coming in!" Marcus waited for a reply but heard none. He should wait for back up but Allie had been trapped with this man long enough. Marcus turned and kicked the door open. Wood pieces chipped off the door frame and fell to the floor.

Slowly, he made his way through the first level of the house. No sign of him. Surely they hadn't left already. Marcus made his way up the stairs without a sound. He searched the first two bedrooms, no sign of life anywhere. Where could they be hiding?

One more floor to clear. If they weren't on

the third floor, Allie had slipped through his fingers yet again. He heard his phone vibrating. He paused and silenced it before going back up the stairs. Marcus swung the door open wide, gun ready to fire. He stepped into the room and turned to find Bastian holding a knife to Allie's throat.

"Bastian, drop the knife."

"Never. She's mine. She's not leaving me. She doesn't want to leave." Bastian pointed the knife at Marcus. "Put the gun down." The knife went back to Allie's throat.

"You know I can't do that, Bastian. I don't want to hurt you, just let her go." Marcus glanced at Allie.

"Shoot him, Marc."

"What if I miss?"

"Just do it!" She screamed and gasped when

the knife cut into her skin.

"Drop the gun!" Bastian shouted. "I'll kill her!"

"Shoot him, Marc! Now!"

"You shut up!" Bastian yelled in Allie's ear.

"Shoot him! Shoot him!"

Bastian's body tensed. He pulled the knife from Allie's throat to turn it.

Marcus saw his shot and took it.

His bullet pierced Bastian's hand. The knife clattered to the floor. With two gunshot wounds Allie easily had him on the ground in seconds, holding her hand out to him for cuffs.

"Nice shot."

"I was aiming for his head." He teased and handed her the cuffs.

As soon as Bastian was secure, Allie stood

up and wrapped her arms around his neck. Her voice was tearful as sirens filled the air. "I knew you'd find me."

Marcus held her back, brushing the hair from her face. "Always."

Allie glanced over her shoulder at Bastian. "What will happen to him?"

"What?"

"I mean, he can't be executed, right?"

"He killed Carly."

"Everyone wanted to; he just got to it first."

Was she making excuses for this guy? Marcus heard his name being called behind him. He put his arm around Allie's shoulders and walked her outside. After spending so much time with him, it was possible Allie had begun to develop some feelings for Bastian. Had he been too late?

*****

Allie lay back on the hospital bed, staring at the square ceiling tiles. The door opened and she let her head fall to the side to see who came in.

Nate limped in wearing a black pinstripe three piece suit. Her heart skipped a beat. "You've moved from one bed to another but you're still chained down."

"I guess so. Is it true? Did you kill those people?" Allie's hand reached for the call button for the nurse and secured it in her grip.

"Well, you don't beat around the bush." Nate pulled a chair up next to the bed and sat down. "Yes I did." He reached over to the outlet on the wall where the call button was connected. He jerked the cord from the wall and smiled. "Sorry, I prefer privacy."

"So this is it, then? You're going to kill me?"

Nate frowned. "I only kill the people I'm told to."

"Are you psycho?" Allie shook her head, raising her hands to cover her face. "Nate, you've murdered four people!"

His laugh was without humor. "Oh I've killed a lot more than four."

She looked back at him. He sat staring at his hands. His thumb rubbed the palm of his left hand as if trying to get something off. "Why are you telling me this?"

"I want you to know the truth." He glanced over his shoulder. "I've thought long and hard about this and the time has come. I need an ally."

"I'm not going to help you kill, Nate, or help

you get away with it. In fact, stick around because Marcus should be back any minute."

"No, actually, he's been delayed." Nate shrugged. "Sorry, habit."

Her eyes grew large. "What did you do to him?"

"Oh relax, he's locked in the bathroom." Nate chuckled and shook his head. "He's really going to hate me now."

"So am I. What do you want, Nate?"

"I killed Katie." Nate reached into his coat pocket and pulled out a piece of notebook paper. "I didn't mutilate her. That's not my style and *that's* why I joined your unit." He held the paper out to her. "This is who I think mutilated Katie."

Allie took the paper and unfolded it. "Elaine Meek? The wife of the CEO? What does she have to do with it?"

"She's the one that hired me to kill Katie. Katie was having an affair with Henry."

"Henry's dead." Her eyes grew large. "Don't tell me you killed him too."

"Yeah, I did." Nate winced. He held up his hand to stop her from talking. "But she told me to do that too."

"You expect me to believe a murderer?"

"No, I expect you to believe a friend. I wouldn't lie about this Allie." He stood up and moved his chair back. "I'm glad you're all right."

"Why don't you turn yourself in?"

Nate scoffed. "I'd be dead within fifteen minutes. I won't let arrest me. If I have to die, I'll do it my way." Nate limped to the door. "Run down that lead and you'll have your answer, I promise."

"What about your other victims?"

"They were all rich, entitled animals. They deserved what they got; Katie didn't."

*****

"After a day like this, I could sure use some Chinese. How about you?" Marcus sat down next to her on the hospital bed.

"Are you buying?"

"Me? Do you have any idea the trouble I went through trying to find you? Let alone being locked in the bathroom for a good thirty minutes thanks to your pal."

"My pal?"Allie laughed and took his hand. "He's hardly my pal, but I'm glad I got stuck with you."

"Me too." Marcus glanced up at the TV as the news came on showing Allie's rescue, followed by the arrest of Elaine Meek. "Look at that. I'm a hero. Who would have thought?" Marcus winked at her.

"Yes, my hero in navy Kevlar." Allie patted his shoulder. Marcus had rescued her and Nate had rescued Katie.

Wherever he was, she hoped he could see the news. There had been something in his voice when he'd talked about her, like he'd known her.

She was still baffled by his admission of the killings. He only killed the people he was told to kill. What was that supposed to mean? He was forced to be a contract killer?

"So are you still leaving me or have you decided you might stick around awhile?" Marcus' question interrupted her thoughts.

Allie sighed and looked down at her wrists

rubbed raw from the handcuffs. Nate had escaped.

She couldn't leave with his case file still open, no

matter how many of his client names he turned over

to her.

With Bastian out of the picture, there was no

reason for her to leave. Allie met Marcus' eyes. "I

guess I could stick around for awhile."

Marcus stood quickly and moved to the

window. "I knew you couldn't live without me." He

said smugly. He turned on his heel and frowned,

motioning toward the hospital bed. "What are you

still doing here? Let's go!"

"I'm waiting for the doctor to say I can

leave."

"He already did. I told you, he prescribed

you Chinese food and the company of a charming

friend."

Allie laughed and nodded. "All right and where am I supposed to get the charming friend?"

A look of mock pain crossed his face. "That cuts me to the core. I'll forgive you though since you're paying." Marcus winked and headed for the door. "I'll be waiting out here."

Allie took her clothes and went to the bathroom to change. It was odd to think everything had ended so quickly. The week she'd spent with Bastian had seemed to last forever. He was in jail now; right where he belonged.

She looked in the mirror, her finger tracing the cut on her forehead, eternal evidence of what had happened to her. Death in the line of duty had become a family legacy. She'd managed to cheat death once more. How many more lives did she have?

About Rae

Rae Burton is an award winning mystery author from the Midwest. She enjoys writing mystery and suspense novels, as well as some historical romances. Currently she is working on the second installment of The Krenshaw Files.

Coming November 2015:

~Only the Elect are taken~

**Families are the target and it's up
to Detective Allie Krenshaw to put a
stop to the killing spree.**

Made in the USA
San Bernardino, CA
11 October 2015